For Nina Landay Stuart,
who, for as much as she loves labels,
cannot be defined by one.
&
My nieces: Maisie, Lili, Mia & Phoebe,
who fill the daughter-shaped hole in my heart.

You are SO NOT INVITED to my BAT MITZVAH!

FIONA ROSENBLOOM

LITTLE, BROWN AND COMPANY
New York Boston

Copyright © 2023 by Alloy Entertainment and Fiona Rosenbloom

Cover art copyright © 2023 by Neil Swaab
Cover design by Neil Swaab and Gabrielle Chang
Cover copyright © 2023 by Hachette Book Group, Inc.
Interior design by Michelle Gengaro

Image credits: page i: © Grandview Graphics/Shutterstock.com;
chapter openers: © irkus/Shutterstock.com

Little, Brown and Company
Hachette Book Group
1290 Avenue of the Americas, New York, NY 10104
Visit us at LBYR.com

Originally published in hardcover and ebook by Hyperion,
an imprint of Disney Book Group, in September 2005
First Trade Paperback Edition: April 2007
Movie Tie-In Edition: July 2023

Little, Brown and Company is a division of Hachette Book Group, Inc.
The Little, Brown name and logo are trademarks of Hachette Book Group, Inc.

The publisher is not responsible for websites
(or their content) that are not owned by the publisher.

Little, Brown and Company books may be purchased in bulk for business, educational, or promotional use. For information, please contact your local bookseller or the Hachette Book Group Special Markets Department at special.markets@hbgusa.com.

Library of Congress Cataloging-in-Publication Data
Names: Rosenbloom, Fiona, author.
Title: You are so not invited to my bat mitzvah / Fiona Rosenbloom.
Description: Revised trade paperback edition. | New York : Little, Brown and Company, 2023. | Originally published in hardcover and ebook by Hyperion, an imprint of Disney Book Group, in September 2005. | Audience: Ages 12 and up. | Summary: As her bat mitzvah approaches, Stacy Adelaide Friedman of White Plains, New York, has a lot on her mind: her parents have separated, her mother dresses her like an American Girl doll, her younger brother is embarrassing, and she is totally in love with Andy Goldfarb.
Identifiers: LCCN 2022057198 | ISBN 9780316565509 (paperback) | ISBN 9780316567060 (ebook)
Subjects: CYAC: Bat mitzvah—Fiction. | Interpersonal relations—Fiction. | Friendship—Fiction. | New York (State)—Fiction.
Classification: LCC PZ7.R7191744 You 2023 | DDC [Fic]—dc22
LC record available at https://lccn.loc.gov/2022057198

ISBNs: 978-0-316-56550-9 (pbk.), 978-0-316-56706-0 (ebook)

Printed in the United States of America

LSC-C

Printing 1, 2023

It is our great pleasure to invite you
to join us when our daughter

Stacy Adelaide Friedman

is called to the Torah as a Bat Mitzvah
Saturday, the fourteenth of May
at nine in the morning

Temple Emanu-El
Purchase, New York

Please join us after for a celebration
immediately following services

Morton Friedman & Shelly Friedman

Prologue
Baruch Ata I Don't Know

Hi, God.

Stacy Adelaide Friedman here.

But you probably already knew that.

So, I guess I'll jump right in.

God (I hope you don't mind if I call you that)—I know you're probably backed up with bat mitzvah season and I don't mean to take you away from all your responsibilities, but I was wondering if I could have a minute of your time.

I'll take that as a yes.

As you know, in just a month, I will be celebrating my bat mitzvah. I am very much looking forward to this joyous occasion, and I'm even excited about becoming an adult, but I have a few concerns regarding this special day, and I thought we should discuss them before it's too late.

My first concern is my Torah portion....

I really think it will sound better if I don't have to SING. I'm an awful singer. I can't carry a tune when I lip-synch! Even my best friend, Lydia, doesn't think I should sing. "Your voice is a mood no one wants to be in." And she thinks I'm good at most everything. Especially telling jokes. So I was thinking that maybe instead of singing my Torah portion the way my bat mitzvah teacher, Rabbi Sherwin, has been teaching me, I could read it, and then to make up for not singing it, I could do a little stand-up. Whaddya think, God?

You don't have to give me an answer

right away. But while you're thinking
about it, let's talk about my dress.... Now,
I know you're not a stylist, but someone
needs to run interference with my mother.
I'm sorry that she and Dad are separated,
but that doesn't mean she has to ruin my
life by dressing me like a 1940s American
Girl character. I'm almost thirteen
years old. I'm not asking to dress like
Addison Rae (and she's not even the most
provocatively dressed TikTok influencer!).
But it'd be nice if I could wear something
short and cool and preferably from Shein
(which my mom says is a "hard pass"
because of sustainability issues, and other
important words I missed because I wasn't
listening).

While you're thinking, I'd also like to
know if Arthur's participation is absolutely
mandatory that day. I know he's my
little brother (though, as you've probably
noticed, he's not so little anymore—he's
almost an entire elementary-school kid

taller than me, and growing), but his presence sends a potentially negative message to my peers, at a particularly crucial time in my social development. Evidence: After he accidentally smacked me in the face, due to his inability to synchronize his gestures with his quickly lengthening limbs, he claimed I have a severe case of congenital amusia, which he insists is not amusing. I finally looked it up. It's just fancy talk for "tone-deaf." So, you understand what I'm getting at, don't you, God?

That's all I really wanted to ask. Not too much, really. Just three tiny favors. Three teeny, tiny little favors. And then I'm all yours. A bat mitzvah. A Jewish young woman ready to do whatever is expected of her by you and yours.

So, see what you can do. And thanks. Okay, God. See you at my bat mitzvah.

Love,

Stacy

PS: Is it okay to add a PS? Because if it is, I'd like to add this:

It's about . . . how do I put this, God? It's . . . it's about a boy.

How are you doing, God?

Are you okay with this so far?

Because I know you have rules about boys.

Hmmm. Maybe you should sit down, God.

Okay. Here goes:

There's this boy in my class. Last year the only time he talked to me or my friends was to ask if we wanted to follow his YouTube channel (we didn't), but then, like the climate, something changed, and this year he just hits different. Who knows why, but whatever the case, he's extra super cute (or as my friend Kelly would say, he's a "whole snack"). His name is Andy Goldfarb (obviously you know who I'm talking about) and I think I'm in love with him, and I know I'm not the only one. He just has this way about him.

I don't know what's happening to me,
God. I've never had this feeling before
and I don't know what to do with myself.
All I know is that I want him to love me
back. So, in addition to finding me a great
dress, I wouldn't argue if you made my
hair less frizzy and my face 40 percent
prettier. Again, not such a huge thing to ask
for compared to what other people want.
(More follows on TikTok. An Oculus Quest
headset. World peace.)

I hope it's not too much trouble.

Thanks again, God.

Really.

See you there!

1.
The Gross Mitzvah

"Well? Am I Andy Goldfarb ready?" I asked. I was standing on the steps of Temple Emanu-El with Lydia Katz and Kelly Mooreland, my absolute first- and second-best friends, in respective order. We were about to enter Marni Gross's bat mitzvah party and I wanted to look amazing.

Kelly stood back and gave me the once-over. "We need to zhuzh your face. You need more attitude. We need makeup."

"My mom does not support me wearing makeup," I complained.

"Not a worry," Kelly said, digging into her purse to show me her Glossier makeup bag.

"Bathroom makeover!" Lydia said, heading toward the synagogue's lecture hall. Lydia knows how to get things done. She's very disciplined. She gets that from her years of ballet classes and all those bunned-up teachers who are constantly waving sticks at dozens of dirty feet. "When we're done with you, you'll forget about Andy Goldfarb. You'll be Dante Decosimo ready," she added.

I rolled my eyes at her. Yeah, right.

Dante Decosimo was the ultra-gorgeous Italian exchange student in our class. He was another level of hot. Like, I wasn't sure I was even allowed to look at him. Even Kym Armstrong, leader of our class's A-list posse, "the Pipers" (the coolest name they think a girl can have), on whose border Lydia and I currently teetered, was openly into him. And she was, well, hard to please. Apparently, Dante had an older, gorgeous girlfriend who wore off-the-shoulder peasant blouses waiting for him back home in Genoa. And rumor had it he'd already hooked up once with some teen model from another school here in Rye.

"Are we ready, ladies?" Kelly asked.

Lydia readjusted her dark brown ballerina bun, straightened her complicatedly crinkled spaghetti-strap dress, and pliéd her feet toes-out (again, the dance training). Kelly flipped her thick blond hair over her back and neatened her tulle-trimmed dress. I made sure the back of my dress wasn't stuck in my tights.

"All signs point to..." I started.

"YES!" we said together.

Then we opened the door to the synagogue. We were here—the party could officially start.

Unfortunately, as soon as I looked out onto the hallway with all its decorations, I was reminded why calling this a "party" would be a challenge. It's next to impossible to turn an outdated phenomenon—in this case, a Harry Potter–themed bat mitzvah party—into a blowout.

"Am I the only one who finds it incongruent to claim an adherence to social justice causes while also blatantly endorsing a writer who problematically challenges the rights of trans women?" Arthur asked no one in particular.

I had forgotten he was behind us. I was so used to him being on my tail all the time, I hardly even thought about how weird it was that he was almost three years younger than me. At ten years old, Arthur had a higher IQ than most members of the SUNY Purchase faculty and a comparable vocabulary. Half the time I had no idea what he was saying. Fine, more than half. This is how I came to realize that when you can't understand something someone is saying, they're either way smarter than you, or they also don't understand what they're saying. Arthur was smarter than me. And our parents. And his teachers. It was mortifying.

As usual, we left him to fend for himself and headed to the restroom.

"I think we should take off our friendship necklaces," Lydia said to me once we got inside the faux-marble bathroom.

"Why?" I asked. We never took off our friendship necklaces.

"The colors just don't look right with our outfits," she said.

I was so short, I had to stand on my tiptoes to see my top half in the mirror.

"She's right," Kelly said, coating her eyelashes with mascara. Kelly didn't have a friendship necklace, but it wasn't because we didn't love her. It was because Lydia and I had been absolute best friends since kindergarten. Before we even knew Kelly. And we weren't only school best friends; we were also Hebrew school best friends. Besides, you can't split two halves of a heart three ways. Kelly didn't really seem to mind. She was pretty confident like that. Besides, she wouldn't have been caught dead in nickel silver.

"You never want to pair neon with pastels," Kelly said, throwing the mascara in her makeup bag. She turned back to the mirror, exposing her mouth full of braces in her reflection, and checked for food particles.

"You're totally right," I said, not wanting to point out how much I actually did not know if she was right, or wrong for that matter. After all, my mother still picked out my clothes, color palette and all.

"I mean, do you think Kerry Washington would be caught dead in a neon-pastel fashion combo?" Kelly asked. Kelly planned on becoming either an actress or a personal shopper.

"You are so pretty, but you're always hiding behind

your hair," Lydia said as she held out her hand, signaling for me to give her the necklace. That was the other thing about Lydia: She was very big sisterly. She always made sure that I felt as good about myself as she did about herself.

"Okay, girls, are we ready to find the Pipers?" Kelly asked, twirling her hair with her fingers. She did that when she was anxious. Lydia was a little nervous too. I could tell because she was swaying softly back and forth, like she was rocking a baby. Ever since the Pipers lost one of their own to a parental job transfer, they were much more open to hanging out with us. And we, well, we'd been hoping to gain access to their inner circle since the day middle school began. So, you can imagine the pressure we were feeling. What we needed was a good stress reliever.

"Why did Adele cross the road?" I asked.

"Why?" Kelly asked.

"To say hello from the other side!" I said, sending Kelly and Lydia into fits of laughter.

That one never fails me. Telling jokes to ease the tension is a specialty of mine. It's one of the reasons I'm considering the field of comedy as a career choice.

"Ok, now we're ready to find the Pipers," I said.

"And the Crew," Kelly said.

"And the Crew," I repeated, instantly regretting it.

"Ugh, the Crew." Lydia rolled her heavily mascara-ed eyes. Lydia, I should mention, was NOT into the Crew (aka boys). I was trying to be sensitive to this, but my own fixation on boys (one in particular) did not help me.

Standing side by side in the doorway of the party hall, decked out and made up, I felt as if Lydia, Kelly, and I were in an Olivia Rodrigo video. I imagined us strutting into the party, artificial wind blowing our hair back while we dance-followed behind Olivia. Seeing us like this would take everyone's breath away. Andy's especially.

But as we crossed the threshold, we couldn't have been less like Olivia Rodrigo's backup dancers. No one really paid much attention. A couple of people waved, but everyone continued to go about their business.

I searched the room, trying to find Andy. Everyone was dancing, though not really *with* each other. More like *at* each other. Most kids were in huddles. One corner was filled with the techies, some of whom were earnest enough to actually be wearing the Harry

Potter wizard hats. Another corner was ironically filled unironically by the loners. But also, no Andy. In fact, I couldn't find any of the Crew. Did they not come? Were they too good for a bat mitzvah party now?

We walked to the dance floor, passing tables set with Ron Weasley napkins and Harry Potter food: Caterpillar Cocoons, Bloody Eyeballs, and Deviled Mice. Marni Gross needed to wake up and smell reality. Not only was Harry Potter so over, but so was J. K. Rowling, according to Arthur, and apparently all of Twitter, which I wasn't even allowed on. Granted, I would have taken Hogwarts Academy over White Plains any day, but not as a theme for a bat mitzvah. I scanned the room again, but still no Crew. Kelly kept fidgeting with her Louis Vuitton bag, making sure everyone could see it and be envious. Lydia was searching the crowd as we walked. Being a tall girl definitely had its advantages.

"There they are!" she said, pointing over everyone's heads.

My heart fluttered, and I swear my palms even sweated a bit. They were here! My hands reflexively rose to pat down any errant frizz as we made our way across the dance floor and toward our destination.

Lydia said, "Pipers!"

My heart dropped with the disappointed realization that it wasn't the Crew she had spotted at all.

Kym Armstrong, Sara Langley, and Megan Riley were huddled in the corner.

"Love the lip," Kym called to Kelly as they stepped aside and opened up their circle to include us.

"Thanks, it's MAC," Kelly answered.

Kym and Sara were wearing color-coordinated color-blocked halter dresses.

"Let me see the color. I bet I could make it," Megan said as Kelly handed her the tube.

Megan was sporting her do-it-yourself fashion look as usual. Today she was wearing plastic shower rings as bracelets.

"Stacy, your hair is getting really long," Sara said.

"Thanks," I responded, preoccupied and craning my neck to see over Lydia toward the drinks table.

"So." Megan looked at me. I turned my attention back from the party. She lifted her arm to snake all her plastic shower hook bracelets back up. "Is tonight the big night?"

"What do you mean?"

"The night where you make it happen with Andy Goldfarb."

"Make what happen?" I asked nervously.

"You know...make him like you."

You can make someone like you?

"He's not even here," I said.

"So, I guess the answer is no."

"I just saw Rob Mancuso and Dante Decosimo in the parking lot, so Andy must be here," Sara said.

"Hey, you could be the first one out of all of us to have a boyfriend!" Megan said.

"Yeah! Totally. So, what are you waiting for, sister?" Sara asked.

"Come on, Stacy, let's do this!" Kym said.

"Now?" I asked.

"No, sis, when we're in high school. Yes, now!" Kym said.

Don't get me wrong: I wanted to be friends with the Pipers. I wanted to be *in* the Pipers, but Kym Armstrong scared me. I thought she was a snob and kind of a queeny jerk. But I also didn't want to be the person to say no to her.

So, I turned around and headed toward the door of the synagogue. The girls were following me, and I was walking as slowly as I could. I guess I was nervous, because I had no idea what to say when we got outside. "Oh, hi, Andy. Everyone, myself included, totally ships us. So, starting right now, you're my boyfriend. Surprise!"

Then, just as I was ready to push the front door open, the DJ started spinning "Uptown Funk" and Lydia, bless her heart, grabbed my shoulders and shrieked. This was her absolute favorite song. This week.

"Let's dance!" she screamed, snatching my hand and leading me back onto the dance floor.

Kelly, Sara, and Megan ran after us and Kym watched from the side, glaring. Lydia had learned the signature moves from the video, created her own choreographed dance, and taught it to us, which is why soon everyone was watching. Including Rabbi Sherwin, who happens to be a very cool rabbi. Even Arthur, who was sitting on a plastic chair in the corner, was bobbing his head, watching us.

And then, dream of all dreams, Andy Goldfarb, Dante Decosimo, and Rob Mancuso pushed their way through the crowd to see what was going on, which made me get into it even more.

I checked to see if Andy—so cute in his suit and beginnings of a tan—had his eyes on me. For a second it seemed as if he did, and I imagined us as a couple walking into my bat mitzvah together. On the dance floor, he would blow everyone's mind with how good a dancer he was, and I could say nonchalantly to anyone who asked about him, "Oh, you mean that guy? Yeah. He's my boyfriend." And then, maybe even in the middle of a dance, a slow one, at my bat mitzvah party, in front of the Pipers, in front of my whole class, Andy Goldfarb would lean down and kiss me. On the lips.

"Cha Cha Slide" cross-faded in, which I took as my cue to hop out. Andy was still standing there with a big smile on his face. I took this as a sign to courage up and began to walk over to him. On my way there I bumped into Dante Decosimo. "You want to make *il trambusto*?" Dante asked, which was kind of strange, since he's way too gorgeous to speak to someone like me.

"Uh, no thanks," I answered. "I'm not hungry." As I got closer to Andy, I noticed he was mouthing the words to "Don't You Worry," and so I said, "Good song, huh?"

"Believe."

Andy was so cool. He knew everything there was to know about clothes and hip-hop. He only wore Stüssy and Supreme. He even had a personalized belt buckle that said *G-Farb*. I wondered if he knew that I could dance to hip-hop. That would definitely impress him.

"You looked dope out there," he said.

Oh.

My.

God.

He *was* watching me.

Play it cool, Stace.

"Thanks," I said as nonchalantly as I could. Then added, "Wanna dance?" not sure what had possessed me to do such a thing.

But just then, Andy pulled out his cell phone, looked at the text, chuckled, and said, "Dig, I gotta run outside fo' a minute. Chill, a'ight, fam?"

"That's cool," I said. And then "Psychofreak" by Camila Cabello came on. Lydia and Kelly and the other girls screamed again. Lydia ran and grabbed me just as Andy turned away.

We all followed Kelly now. We were all legs and shoulders and I hoped that our un-choreographed choreographed dance made me look as cool as I felt. I imagined Andy watching from the corner, awed at how good I looked. But when I spun around, I saw that he had returned and was now talking to Julie Haven!

Julie Haven was pretty and tall, but she had bad opinions. As Andy talked to her, she was kind of moving her hips, like kind of dancing, kind of not, and then he started to swing his arms a little bit. What was he doing? Was he *dancing* with her? I slowed down a little but also tried to act as if I wasn't fixated.

Then, with absolutely no warning whatsoever, Andy Goldfarb bent down and kissed Julie Haven fast and sloppy and then grabbed her hand and the two of them disappeared through the crowd.

I suddenly stopped dancing. I couldn't even move.

As the DJ changed songs, there was a huge crashing sound in the corner. When we all looked over to see what it was, there was Arthur standing over a huge broken platter of wizard celestial cheese balls and spit-wad sandwiches. He must have been trying to do two things at once, something he's not yet coordinated enough to do. In this case, carry something over to his chair.

"Walk much, Arthur?" someone called out.

"My external longitude and my internal cartography are not yet synchronized!" I could hear him shouting as people started laughing. Poor Arthur. His body was growing faster than he could learn how to operate it. He was constantly miscalculating the length of his arms and legs, knocking things over when he meant to pick them up. Worse yet was when he tried to explain this particular predicament, and it came out like a postgraduate student's dissertation title.

Between the humiliation of having the tallest "little" brother in the world and a crush whose heart belonged to another, I could barely keep it together. And as Beyoncé's "Crazy in Love" floated out of the speakers, I broke down, running off the dance floor in tears.

We all assembled in the synagogue bathroom to discuss our next proper course of action. The atmosphere was tense.

Kelly nervously pinched the color back into her cheeks. Megan Riley was on TikTok. Sara Langley, Rye Country Day's Greta Thunberg, sat on the floor, keeping track of the bat mitzvah's environmental violations on the dry-erase board she carried with her everywhere. Kym lifted herself up on the sink and studied everyone, me especially, waiting to see the outcome of my rage, and Lydia anxiously pinned and re-pinned her hair into its bun and I began my normal habit of stress pacing and biting my fingernails.

I did three laps across the tiled floor, and when I finished the fourth, I stopped and swiveled on my heels, and then I slowly and carefully delivered the most important announcement I was to make that week.

"I have something to say," I began.

Everyone stopped and looked at me.

Kym slid down from the sink to get closer to me. Any sign of gossip and Kym's head was practically in your mouth, ensuring she didn't miss a single word.

"I...

Am...

So...

Over...

Andy...

Goldfarb."

There were audible gasps, mainly from Kelly, who believed most dramatic moments were opportunities to practice her acting skills.

"Are you sure?" Lydia asked, her concern palpable.

"Positively sure," I said. "I am officially over Andrew Joshua Goldfarb."

I looked over at Lydia, who seemed to be waiting for me to say something else.

"You know, just because he kissed Julie Haven doesn't mean he doesn't like you," Lydia said. Poor thing. She had a lot of catching up to do when it came to boys.

"Lydia, call it, please," I said.

Lydia looked at her watch. "Stacy Adelaide Friedman's crush on Andrew Joshua Goldfarb has ended. Time of death: 7:02 p.m. Date: Saturday, April ninth."

We all looked at one another.

"Maybe you should say it, just to make it truly official," Lydia said.

Kelly held her hand out to Kym, who rolled her eyes but took it anyway. Then Megan held hands with Sara, and Lydia clutched mine.

"God as my witness, I officially renounce currently dead-to-me Andy Goldfarb. Stacy Friedman's crush on Andy Goldfarb is now legally over." I checked my watch. "New time of death...7:03. Same date," I said.

And everyone answered in unison, "Amen."

2.

The Possible Start
of a New Beginning

Kelly, Lydia, and I stood outside the synagogue to get some air. I didn't want to be anywhere near Andy Goldfarb and Julie Haven, but I couldn't exactly go home two hours early. It would have been way too obvious. Besides, then I would have had to tell my mother what happened.

"So, what should we do?" Kelly asked.

"We could go to the mall!" Lydia suggested.

"How are we going to get to the mall?" I asked.

"We could walk," she replied.

"In these shoes? I don't think so," Kelly said, looking down at her Marc Jacobs heels.

The door to the synagogue flew open. Arthur stormed out, shouting, "My body is in a state of disequilibrium and could use less attention and more patience!" He was holding on to his right arm, which meant that he had probably tripped and fallen. Poor guy. His center of gravity was shifting constantly.

He plopped himself down on the temple steps, took his worn-out and heavily highlighted copy of *101 Brain Teasers for Adults* from his blazer pocket, and disappeared into the comforting creases of his high IQ.

We turned back around, ignoring him. "I know!" Lydia gasped. "We could sneak back into the party and steal champagne from the kitchen!"

"But then we'd have to go back in there," I said.

"I'll go," Lydia offered.

"I heard that all the bubbles in champagne make you fart a lot," I added. Lydia and Kelly looked at me and burst out laughing.

"Well, that's what I heard!" I said.

We were all racking our brains, thinking of how

we could kill the time, when Andy Goldfarb's brother, Adam, pulled up in his Saab.

"*Hola, guapas y feo,*" he said, leaning out the window.

"*Hola, Adám. ¿Cómo está usted? La fiesta de Marni ha sido encantador. Una bandeja de* celestial cheese balls *cayó al piso de mi mano, pero no era mi culpa,*" Arthur responded.

We turned and stared at Arthur.

"*¿Qué?*" he asked.

"You guys coming to the quarry with us?" Adam asked, ignoring Arthur.

The quarry was where all the cool kids went, including the Pipers and the Crew. It wasn't that far away, but it was difficult to find, and while it was a public swimming hole, the popular kids had made it a very exclusive one.

"When?" Kelly asked.

"Now," Adam answered.

"But the party's not over yet," Kelly added.

"The party is just about to start," Adam answered.

"No, we're not coming," Kelly said. "We're just getting some air."

"There's this new thing where they have air everywhere now. Even at the quarry. Come with us, it'll be straight fire."

Straight fire.

We all looked at one another, uncertain.

"I don't know," Lydia said. "What have we got to lose but a few more hours of sleep?"

"You know, I read, and I'm quoting here, that neuroscientists now believe sleep is not only crucial to brain development but is also necessary to help consolidate the effects of waking experience," Arthur called to us from the steps. "Meaning, of course, memory integration."

We ignored him as Kym Armstrong, Megan Riley, and Sara Langley walked out of the synagogue with Dante, Rob, and Andy. They all headed over to Adam, who was getting out of his Saab.

"You betties coming with?" Andy asked.

"Yes, they come with us," Dante answered.

"Yeah, come with us," Sara Langley added excitedly.

Arthur suddenly stood up, walked down the steps toward us, and, speaking directly to Sara Langley, said, "On the other hand, the creator of the Wim Hof Method has successfully healed his body using cold water immersion. Not that I'm advocating that, or dispensing medical advice of any sort, just reiterating what I've read. Not to mention—"

"You're not coming with us, Arthur," I interrupted.

"That is inaccurate. You are my official point of contact this evening, my warden, my custodian, my metaphysical curator of time, if you will…" he responded.

"What do you guys think?" I asked the girls.

"I definitely don't think he should come," Kelly agreed.

"No, not about him, about going to the quarry," I said. I knew I wasn't going to be able to shake Arthur.

"Oh," Kelly said, and looked at the Crew and then the Pipers. They were waiting on our answer.

"C'mon, fam, what's it going to be?" Andy asked.

And before I could stop myself, I blurted, "We're going."

"Heard," Adam said.

3.
Two Cigarettes, Six Beers & a Dare

Even though I had renounced Andy, I still tried to follow him up the rock face. But Dante kept on getting in front of me. Watching Dante walk up a hill wasn't exactly a prison sentence, but even so, I wanted to be closer to Andy. Especially considering that Julie Haven wasn't here.

STACY FRIEDMAN'S STATEMENT OF FACT REGARDING MATTERS OF LOVE: Sometimes when you publicly renounce a boy, you realize that privately, you still love him.

I was trying so hard to maneuver around Dante that I slipped and fell, scraping my knee. Dante bent down and examined my wound, while Andy and the other boys just kept on walking. Not once looking back.

"No broken bones, just the blood," he said. Then he dug through his pockets and pulled out a fancy handkerchief that had his name delicately embroidered in blue and held it to my knee.

"You give it back another time," he said.

Why was Dante so sweet and Andy so...not? How could he ignore something as crucial as a bleeding leg? Maybe he was too busy thinking about Julie Haven and her wrong opinions to be concerned with certain life-or-death situations involving me!

We continued the climb with Adam leading. When we finally reached flat rock, the Crew ripped off their shirts and jumped off into the water below. They were whooping and hollering and we and the Pipers were just sitting on the rock face, watching. Adam opened a beer, sucked it down, and then lit a cigarette. When my cell phone vibrated I knew it had to be my mother calling. I simply had to be *in proximity* to beer and cigarettes and her superhero sense-detector would go off.

The Crew came back up, wet and dripping water on us. Andy shook his head over us and yelled, "Boo-yah!" and we got sprayed. If ever there was holy water, that must have been it. All the girls shrieked and tried to dry off, but not me. I wanted that water to stay on my arms forever.

I wondered why Julie Haven was good enough for Andy to kiss her but not good enough to be invited to the quarry.

"Aren't you guys coming in?" Rob asked.

"Yes, the quarry swimming is a refresh," Dante said.

"We have no bathing suits," Kelly said.

"So?" Andy said.

"So, we're not going in naked," Kelly said.

"Who said anything about nekid? Go in your clothes, ain't no federal offense."

"But we're wearing dresses," I said.

"Oh, come on. You came all the way here and now you won't go in the water?" Rob asked.

"Yeah, at least one of you has to go in," Adam said.

"Pipers, a conference," Kym called.

We walked a few feet away from the Crew and stood in a small circle.

"Should we go in?" Kym asked.

"I'm not really a good swimmer," Megan argued.

"That's true, I've seen her. People drown with more grace," Sara agreed.

Megan glared at her.

"Well, what about you, Kelly?" Kym asked.

"Do you know how long it took me to do my hair? Hard pass," Kelly said.

"Sara?"

"I have my period, and you can't swim with your period," she answered, and then stared down, clearly hoping no one would call her out on this blatant lie.

Kym then looked at me.

"My mom will kill me if she sees me with wet hair," I said.

"True, her mom is really strict," Lydia said.

"So what's your excuse, Lydia?" Kym asked haughtily.

"I don't have one," Lydia said.

"Then I don't see any reason for you not to be the one to go in, unless, of course, your reason is that you don't like boys."

Kym was always taunting Lydia for not being

overtly into boys, as though that were Lydia's only dating option. It was infuriating, and as Arthur would say, so *heteronormative*. Somehow it offended Kym's sense of the way seventh-grade girls should be. I mean, I was a late bloomer also, but she left me alone because she knew I loved Andy. She couldn't pick on Kelly, either, because in sixth grade Kelly went on a date with Lucas Pennington.

"I like boys just fine," Lydia announced.

"And yet, no boyfriend," Kym said, putting her hands on her hips. "How interesting."

Megan kicked at a rock. Lydia's face was in a grimace. I started biting my fingernails. Kelly turned her head back and forth between them, studying their facial expressions for future acting experience.

"Your boyfriend's name is on the tip of my tongue," Lydia said, pretending to think. "Don't tell me. I just remembered—his name is *You Don't Have One Either*."

She was a natural at the comeback.

"Is that a yes or a no to swimming?" Kym asked Lydia.

We looked back and forth from Kym to Lydia until

finally Lydia kicked off her flats and said, "Fine, I'll do it."

"You can't just jump in wearing your dress!" I said.

"Well, she can't exactly take it off!" Kelly said.

We walked back to the Crew, who were standing cross-armed and shivering. Andy's teeth were chattering, and his lips were blue.

"Who's it going to be?" he said through his smashing teeth. Without missing a beat, Lydia handed me her purse and jumped off the side of the rock face in her complicatedly crinkled dress and into the water. The rest of us just stood and stared at one another.

Then my cell phone vibrated again, and again, I ignored it. Finally, I took my friendship necklace out of Lydia's bag and put it back on, just to keep from dying of boredom. The swimmers had been down there a long while. We could hear them laughing and screaming. Soon we heard voices coming closer, but the only people to appear on the rocks were Dante and Rob. Andy and Lydia were still in the water, but it was quiet.

I wondered if Arthur had found some rare strain of bark on the way up the rock face and was testing the chemical compounds for extra credit in science or something. What the hell was taking him so long?

"Do you hear that?" I asked the girls.

"Hear what?" Kym answered.

"There's no noise. You think they're okay?"

All the girls sort of rushed to the edge of the rock face. We lay on our stomachs and looked down but couldn't see them.

"Lydia?" I yelled down. But there was no answer. I was really starting to freak out. I edged out farther along the rock so my whole head was hanging over.

"LYDIA! LYDIA! ARE YOU OKAY?" I screamed. Then I looked at Kym.

"If she's hurt or dead, this is all your fault!" I yelled at Kym, who suddenly looked panicked. Then the Crew rushed to the edge and hung their heads over. We all started yelling, "LYDIA?! ANDY?!"

But there was nothing. A minute later, I heard laughing and splashing. "I'M FINE!" she yelled back up at us, but before I had the chance to respond, we heard this bizarre noise, this heaving. I turned around and watched as a shape appeared over the flat rock. It looked like the back of someone's head. Then the back of someone's sweat-drenched oxford shirt, then legs. Arthur turned around to face us and stood triumphant on the quarry top, breathing heavily as sweat dripped down the front of his shirt. "I made it!" he said, beaming with pride. "I walked up backward. It challenges the brain to make new neural connections. I think I can feel them forming!"

"It's time to go, neuron," I said, which was true. It was almost nine o'clock, which was when the bat mitzvah was scheduled to end. We all shuffled past Arthur, pushing him out of the way as we started back down to Andy and Lydia.

I carried Lydia's shoes and her bag and handed them to her. She stood near the edge of the rock face and was wringing out the front of her skirt. I walked around her and twisted the back of it, getting out as much water as I could.

"Thanks, you," she said.

Then we all climbed down the rock again, with Adam taking the lead. This time I didn't fall, and Arthur didn't walk backward. Thank you, Yahweh.

At the bottom of the quarry, we walked the long path that led back to the synagogue parking lot. I had ended up walking with Andy completely by luck and some quick choreography. Could he not feel the wrongness of Julie's opinions when he kissed her? She thought COVID was a hoax! Real people real died, and she questioned its legitimacy! How could you want to kiss a person like that? I wanted to know whether he was going to ask her out, and if so, why was I there but she wasn't?

Don't ask him, I thought. *DO NOT ASK HIM ANYTHING ABOUT JULIE HAVEN. IT WILL SEEM DESPERATE AND NEEDY AND WILL PUSH HIM AWAY FOREVER.*

DO!

NOT!

ASK!

HIM!

ABOUT!

JULIE!

HAVEN!

"So, I didn't know you and Julie Haven were friends," I said.

Way to go, self.

"Yeah, pawtna, she's mad fine."

Then a long and excruciating silence stretched out between us as we walked slowly across the parking lot. Mad fine? She was NOT mad fine. She IS an anti-vaxxer!

KISS ME! I thought. *I'M SORRY I RENOUNCED YOU. I UN-RENOUNCE YOU. IF ONLY YOU WOULD RENOUNCE JULIE HAVEN!*

As we neared the synagogue, I turned to make sure that Arthur was still with us. Lydia, who was being awfully quiet, was trailing almost as far behind everyone as Arthur was.

I turned back as we approached the parking lot and saw Julie Haven sitting on the synagogue steps. I tried not to make eye contact with her, but she was staring right at me. As we got closer, she stood up and ran toward Andy.

"There you are!" she called to him, and glared at me. "Why didn't you wait for me?" she asked him. "I thought we were going to the quarry." He didn't answer as she slipped her arm through his and led him away from all of us. I tried to meet Lydia's eyes, but she was staring, mouth open, at Andy and Julie. I loved that she was just as angry with him for not loving me as I was.

Kym put her finger down her throat, mock puking at Julie Haven and Andy. I forced a smile.

Well, I guess that's that, I thought. I was back where I started: I was letting Andy Goldfarb go. Renounced, un-renounced, and renounced again.

So much for second chances.

4.

Dress Me Up in Yarmulkes

Where ARE you, God? Are you in another store? I need help here. I'm stuck in a dressing room at the White Plains Galleria because I am trapped in a dress! Not just any dress, but the most perfect gold pleated dress. Well, perfect, except two sizes too small!

I felt a small draft and heard my mother say: "Oh my gosh, Stacy Adelaide Friedman! What have you done?"

"Mom, please get out of here!" I shrieked. As I was removing it, the dress had caught itself right below my rib cage. Now my arms were crossed above my head and pinned against my face, and the hard buttons were pressing themselves into my eyelids—I couldn't see a thing.

My mother stepped all the way into the dressing room and grabbed a handful of the material and tried to pull it over my head. This did not help.

"Ow! Omigod, stop!" I said.

She tried to push my arms back through the armholes.

"MOTHER! Stop it, please. You're making it worse," I said.

"I never should have let you try on this dress," she said. "Excuse me, yoo-hoo! Can I get some assistance?" she yelled as she ran after some poor unsuspecting salesperson.

I began losing circulation in my right arm while my mother went to get the nearest dress surgeon. Kelly had the decency to stand outside the dressing room door.

"Can I see what you look like?" Kelly asked.

"NO!" I shrieked, and tried to keep the curtain

flush against the wall with my hip, secured (I hoped) by my foot. The dress was essentially upside-down while I was caught inside it, and my belly and underwear were exposed. My body started to get cold while my face started to sweat. If Lydia were here, I bet she would have positioned my body into some complicated dance move and slipped me right out of this predicament. But, as always, she was at ballet.

"Come on, just a peek. I need it for research," Kelly said.

"What research? You've never researched anything in your life," I said.

"It's acting research. What if I have to play a character who gets stuck in a dress?"

"It's called imagination," I said as my mother and the salesperson suddenly came running back, armed with scissors. The salesperson began pulling, twisting, and snipping at the dress. The way she was shoving me about made me wonder if she understood that I was still in it. My mother was no help.

"What about from that angle?" she asked the salesperson. "Try cutting it from over there," she added. But the salesperson continued to ignore my mother until the dress finally fell off me, along with about a tablespoon of my hair. Then she handed it to my mother and hurried out of the room. My mother looked at the price tag and paled.

"Two hundred and twenty dollars, Stacy! What if they make us pay for this? This is a *shandeh*," my mother said.

Oh, so now she was invoking Yiddish? Why couldn't she just use the word *outrage*, like a normal mother? Ever since she and my dad decided to separate, she's been throwing herself into knitting and Judaism the way I wished Andy Goldfarb would throw himself at me.

"I'm sorry. I didn't get stuck on purpose."

I was now so cold, my goose bumps were starting to burn.

"Who spends that kind of money on a dress?"

"Kylie Jenner?" I asked.

"What are we going to do with a cut-up dress?"

"Make yarmulkes?" I answered.

My mother gave me a long, hard glare. "I woke up with one nerve this morning and you are using it, Stacy Adelaide Friedman."

Just then her phone rang. Which was great because I needed a break from her overused nerve.

"Hello?" she snapped.

Then: "Oh, hello," she practically sang.

When her speaking voice changed octaves, I knew instantly it was my father.

I started to get dressed, but my mother vigorously shook her head, indicating that we were not done trying on dresses. Hallelujah!

Separation or no separation, my mother still loved my father a lot. She loved him as much as Arthur loved adult brainteasers, as much as Kelly loved Kerry Washington and designer clothes, as much as Lydia loved ballet, and as much as I loved Andy Goldfarb. "We're at the Galleria, trying to find Stacy her dress. (*Pause*.) Well, it's going just great, thank you," she said, her eyes still fixed on the price tag for the dress.

"I'm not sure how long I'll be...What? Oh. Okay, that soon? No, no, that's fine. No problem. We'll be there."

Then my mother clicked off her phone and ran out of the dressing room. Moments later she returned with a red face and a hurried, maniacal stare, frantically waving a dress that looked like a good choice for wallpaper in a classroom at a clown-training academy. It was shapeless, with abstract splotches splotching about in every imaginable color. It looked like the colors of the rainbow had decided to split up to start their own rainbows and were now frantically racing around to try and find their new spot.

"Try this on," she said, thrusting it at me.

"You're kidding me, right?" I asked.

"Do I look like I'm kidding, Stacy? We have no time for this. Your father is dropping Arthur off in an hour and I need to shower, change, and have dinner on the table before he arrives. You will try this on and if it fits, we will buy it. Are we clear?"

She was acting a little uncorked, and I knew why. It was because she was hoping my dad would stay for Shabbat dinner. He stayed one Friday night a month ago, and ever since then, she'd been hoping he'd do it again. But he hadn't. I think he only stayed because there was a storm and the roads were slick. But I don't think my mom realized that.

The dress looked like a non-precocious child had decorated and designed it. As if the abstract colorful shapes weren't making themselves clear, it also had beaded appliqué trim and a metallic organza bow. I tried it on and checked myself out in the mirror. I looked like a second grader's knapsack.

"Perfect," my mother declared. "We're getting it."

Kelly's jaw dropped.

"Perfect?" I said. "Perfect? Mom, no. If there's a *shandeh* to be had, then this is it. This is the *shandeh*. Mom, this dress is repulsive, no offense to the person who made it, but no. Hard pass. No one gets dressed up to glow *down*."

"This one's fine. We're getting it," my mother repeated as she stood up.

"I don't want fine!" I screamed at her.

She whipped around and turned to me, speaking in her witch's whisper. "Listen, young lady, you behave yourself. You might be able to speak to your father like this, but not to me. Are we clear?"

Tears started to fall down my cheeks as I pictured myself at my bat mitzvah wearing this dress. Everyone would laugh. I would become so flustered, I would forget how to read Hebrew. I would drop the Torah. The pictures would have to be burned as soon as they were taken. My entire life would unravel just as I was embarking on adulthood. I wouldn't be surprised if Birthright rejected me before I even applied. It would be a daymare.

> *God! 911! Please pick up on this*
> *transmission. WHERE ARE YOU? Are*
> *you even listening to me, God?*

My mother rushed to the register, threw her credit card at the cashier, and pointed at me.

"It's for that. We're getting that dress," she said.

"Mom, I am begging you. Please don't do this to me." But she just ignored me.

"What a beautiful dress! So, you'll be wearing it home?" the cashier asked.

"NO!" I said. "I am not wearing this home."

"Yes," my mother said to the lady as she signed the sales slip, "she'll wear the dress home."

"Mother!"

"Stacy, I don't have time now to wait around for you to change. Your father is on his way. Now let's go!"

My mother took her copy of the receipt, shoved it

into her purse, which was overflowing with yarn from her latest project, and raced out of the store toward the escalator. Kelly and I jogged lightly to keep up with her.

"Mom, can you slow down a little, please?" I called. She just kept on going and we huffed and puffed behind her, me still in just my socks and...oh no, I could feel a joke forming. What's blue and green and yellow and orange and black and red and purple and brown and teal and aqua? THIS DRESS. Kelly was carrying my shoes and school clothes, but I could feel her keeping as much distance as possible.

Look away! I wanted to scream at children as they passed. *Shield your irises!*

We were almost to the down escalator when I heard a commotion. I turned around to see who was making it, and to my utter horror I saw Andy Goldfarb, Rob Mancuso, and Dante Decosimo getting off the up escalator and walking RIGHT TOWARD US.

"Damn, dawg," Andy Goldfarb called, snapping the air a few times as he saw me from fifty feet away. "You a bridesmaid of your frenemy?"

I was mortified, stung. I had no choice now but to stop. I couldn't pretend that they hadn't seen me. Could

I? Rob Mancuso laughed, and Dante, always a few languages behind, looked utterly perplexed.

"What is frenemy?" Dante asked.

That did it. The bat mitzvah was canceled. Despite my incapacitating phone shyness, I'd call everyone myself. Even my mother's friends.

"Aren't you guys supposed to be at tennis?" Kelly asked as she cocked her head the way she did when she was flirting.

"Ain't you heard? Coach Welling kicked it with some raw meat last week and nephew's got E. coli hella bad."

My mother was already standing by the elevator. When she saw us talking with the Crew, she stormed her way back over to us.

"Girls!" my mother yelled at us. As if we were alone and in the privacy of our own home. "Let's get a move on!" When she reached us, she stared disdainfully at Andy's latest baggy getup, then at her watch.

Now I was actually grateful my mom was in such a hurry to leave. At least it gave me an exit strategy.

"Well, guys," I said, looking at the floor. "Gotta go."

"This shopping hall is very luxurious," Dante said,

completely ignoring my exit line and opening up a whole new round of conversation. Which just translated into more time for everyone to view my dress. He offered his hand to my mother. "It is lovely to meet the mother of Stacy."

My mother smiled, then opened her mouth to respond. But nothing came out. She was seemingly rendered speechless by his impeccable manners. He could have said, "Stacy quit school nine weeks ago and just pretends to go," and it wouldn't have mattered.

"Dante!" a male voice called. We all turned as a man, weighed down by two oversized Barnes & Noble bags, came careening toward us.

"Meester Weiss!" Dante called as the man did a double take at my mother.

"Meesus Friedman, I'd like you to meet my father host, Meester Weiss."

Mr. Weiss had a mop of salt-and-pepper hair and thick tortoiseshell glasses. He reminded me of the intellectuals my mother liked to hear "give a talk" at the library. His smile was genuine, and he shook my mother's hand and met her eye.

"Hello," he said.

"Hello," my mother said, a little too cold for my taste.

The man looked at the Crew.

"Are we ready?"

The Crew nodded.

"We're going to Friendly's. Can I interest any of you in a soda?" he asked.

"A lovely invitation, but we need to be home before sundown for the Jewish Sabbath. Nice to meet you, though," my mother said.

"Alan. Alan Weiss. Good Shabbos." He said *Shabbos* instead of *Sabbath.* Wow. Only people who've actually celebrated Shabbos call it that.

"Okay, Alan. Bye now."

"Well, see ya," I said to the Crew, but fixing my final gaze on Andy.

"A'ight, pawtna. Good luck witcha bridesmaids." He laughed at his own joke, then said to me, "I'll give you a holla. Kickin' it at my crib all weekend, company style."

The lump in my throat started to relax. *Did he just*

invite me over to his house? I wondered as my mother grabbed my hand and pulled me away.

By the time I got to the parking lot, the horror at what had just happened began to sink in.

"He called me an ugly bridesmaid!" I said to Kelly as we rushed across the parking lot, trying to keep up with my mother.

"No he didn't."

I stopped cold in my tracks.

"Did you not hear what he said to me, Kelly?"

"I did, but he didn't say ugly. It was kinda funny."

"It wasn't funny to me," I said.

"Well, you gave him up, so what do you care anyway?"

I continued walking.

"What do you think he meant when he said he was 'kickin' it at my crib all weekend'?"

"You didn't give him up at all, did you?" Kelly asked.

"Well, I only gave him up because he gave me up.

But if he hasn't given me up, then I won't give him up either," I said. "So, do you think he was trying to get me to hang out with him this weekend?"

"Maybe," Kelly said. Why couldn't she have said something a little more helpful than "maybe"?

My mother unlocked the car with her key ring from two hundred feet away. "He should not talk that way," she said, now in a light jog. "It's cultural appropriation."

She got so sanctimonious when she was stressed. Besides, I didn't see how it was cultural appropriation. That's just how cool kids talk. I mean, right?

She glanced at her watch, and started to run. This new Sabbath thing was getting out of hand. Since when did we EVER get home before the sun went down?

If anyone should be running, it should be me, I thought. As far away from my mother as possible.

5.

The Serial Shiksa

The look of horror on Arthur's face would have been slapstick funny were it not for the reason behind it. And no, amazingly, it had nothing to do with the dress.

Standing in our kitchen, sandwiched between my awkwardly tall, ten-year-old-genius, socially clueless brother and my horn-rimmed, collar-up, golf-playing, plastic surgeon father, was an artificially tanned, Real-Housewives-of-plastic-surgeons-type-looking woman. *There goes the bat mitzvah reconciliation*, I thought.

"Shelly, Stacy—I'd like you to meet Delilah. She's

my new...friend," my father said as he beamed at this woman.

Delilah stuck her long arm straight out. It glowed carroty, like she was one of the major food groups. There was little to no movement in her face when she said, "I've heard so much about you. Both of you."

She had? We'd never heard of her. Was this his girlfriend? How could he already have a girlfriend? He still had a wife. And why didn't her cheeks move when she smiled? Or her forehead?

"Delilah." My mother repeated.

"So nice to *finally* meet you," Delilah said.

Finally? How long had this been going on?

"I thought it was a bonding day for just you and Arthur," my mother said to my father.

"It was, but we got lucky, right, pal?" My dad looked at Arthur. "Delilah made a surprise appearance."

"I thought it was time to meet the kids," she said.

We looked at my dad, who shrugged sheepishly.

My dad was a very good plastic surgeon who was excellent at cosmetic procedures, but he seemed to have had a very heavy hand when it came to Delilah's face. I assumed this was his handiwork. Had he been making some sort of point about age? I didn't get it. It looked rather painful.

My mother and I just nodded, cocking our heads to get a better angle. I felt bad for Delilah. But I felt worse for my mom.

"I love your dress," Delilah added.

"Thank you. I guess," I said.

"It's very flattering. Are you going to wear it for your bar mitzvah?" she asked, trying to get a conversation going.

"Not if I can help it. And it's a *bat* mitzvah."

"Excuse me?"

"It's a *bat* mitzvah. Not a *bar*. Bar mitzvahs are for boys," I told her.

"Right. I keep forgetting. Morty has to keep explaining."

Morty?

Finally, Arthur stepped away from them and tried to slink over to us. My father leaned toward him.

"How about a goodbye for your old man, buddy?"

"You're leaving?" my mother asked.

"Yes. We have reservations."

"La Salle," Delilah boasted.

La Salle? That was the restaurant my father and mother went to all the time.

My father turned beet red. "Old habits die hard?" he said.

"We were hoping you'd stay for dinner," I said.

"Another time, sweet pea," my dad responded.

Arthur tried to slowly sneak away.

"Goodbye, Arthur," my father said.

"Bye, Dad," Arthur called, trying to scamper upstairs before things got any more uncomfortable. I, on the other hand, was a sucker for drama. Especially when it wasn't my own. I was going to stick around.

"Are you going to say goodbye to Delilah?" my dad called to Arthur as he put his arm around her like that's where it belonged.

Arthur stopped in his tracks. "Bye, Delilah..." he squeaked.

STACY FRIEDMAN'S STATEMENT OF FACT FOR PARENTS WHO DATE: If you must start dating someone new, learn this, if you learn anything at all: *Don't spring them on us and pretend it's a gift. Tell us and we'll tell YOU when it's time to meet.*

Arthur finally escaped to the safety of his makeshift science lab, aka his bedroom.

"Well, I don't mean to keep you waiting. If you have reservations, then you should go," my mother said with a not-so-faint edge of hostility.

"So glad we got a chance to stop by," Delilah said with a bit too much enthusiasm for my taste.

"Okay. Great. Well, I need to get dinner on the table; I guess we'll need one less plate. So, Mort, if you'll excuse me..." My mother trailed off.

There were some more awkward exchanges of cheek kissing, handshaking, and then, when the door was shut, my mother turned and fell against it.

"I can't believe he's not staying for dinner," she said, incredulous. "After all that rushing and worrying." My mother looked as if she might cry. Then she started moving about in the foyer, picking up keys and opening drawers and putting things away and rearranging them like some cleaning fanatic. She picked up her latest half-knit creation and set it down again.

"He'd rather take that non-Jew, that shiksa, to *our* restaurant!" she continued.

I watched my father through the side window walking hand-in-hand with Delilah, and I realized that when people separate, it's not always mutual.

"I can't believe he has a girlfriend. I mean, you'd think he'd give it a little time. We've only been separated five months. I did not appreciate that at all."

"Did he say he was going to stay for dinner?" I asked.

She started banging the pillows on the love seat to fluff them up, how she did before company came over. I had never seen her do this when no one was coming. I felt that she needed a friend, so in my best grown-up you-can-confide-in-me voice, I asked, "Are you getting divorced?"

My mother spun around, fear and venom filling her eyes. Uh-oh. This was not the right thing to say. She then spoke in the voice I dreaded most: the one with no inflection. The flat voice.

"Get ready for dinner. Out of that dress."

"I didn't mean..."

"Now, Stacy! To your room!"

I backed away, scared of her and sorry that I had said the wrong thing. Even though I hadn't known when I'd said it that it was the wrong thing. I quickly ran up the stairs, tears streaming down my face. I was embarrassed that I had hurt her feelings when I hadn't meant to. Everything was a mess. The hideous dress, that Andy had seen me in it, that my father had a girl-friend, that I never said the right things, that my mother was mad at me...I was just trying to be her friend.

Why did everything have to be so unfair? Was it life that was hard or was it simply being a person that was hard?

6.
The Big What If

On Sunday morning, I got up for my bat mitzvah lesson with Rabbi Sherwin and checked my phone. No missed calls. No missed texts. The weekend was nearly three-quarters over and still nothing from Andy.

Downstairs, my mother and Arthur were in the breakfast nook, eating pancakes.

"Did anyone call me on the landline?" I asked—yes, desperation *does* lead one to ask absurd and nonsensical questions—as I picked up a pancake, folded it like a slice of pizza, and shoved it into my mouth.

"The phone hasn't rung all morning," my mother said.

Arthur pulled the entire plate of pancakes toward him and, while working on some Mensa math and logic puzzles with his right hand, fed himself steadily from the pile of pancakes with his left hand.

"Arthur, please eat slower. You'll get the hiccups," my mother said.

This was true. Arthur always gave himself hiccups from inhaling more air than he did food. But that wasn't his biggest problem. If my mother was going to spend her time worrying about him, the least she could do was get him to be more mindful of his limbs.

"Well, see ya! If anyone calls me, don't forget to write it down," I said as I headed toward the garage to get my bike.

"Not so fast, young lady," my mother said as I was already out of eyeshot.

I stopped.

"Is your room cleaned?"

"Yes," I yelled from down the hall.

"Did you pack the kugel I made for Rabbi Sherwin?"

"Yes, Mother," I said, wishing she would get off this super-Jew kick. "Can I go, please? I'm going to be late."

"Yes, go. But no dillydallying about afterward. I want you to come straight home."

Dillydallying. Oh, Shelly.

I headed toward the garage as the phone rang. My heart suddenly pounded. I turned and quickly shot back toward the kitchen to see if it was for me. But halfway there I heard my mother say "We got a dress..." and knew that it wasn't Andy calling. So I hopped on my bike and headed down Anderson Hill Road toward Temple Emanu-El.

God, how about a little bargain on the Andy Goldfarb beat? I mean, I know I've renounced and reconsidered him twice already, and maybe I should have left him (emotionally) on read, but I couldn't. He's just too cute. I mean, could you? (Okay, maybe YOU could, but you're God. So.)

Given the circumstances, if you have Andy Goldfarb call me, I'll even wear that grotesque abstract explosion of a dress to my bat mitzvah. Of course,

I'll want to have it altered and taken in and most likely I'll have to remove the beaded appliqué trim and the metallic organza bow and see if maybe I can straighten those weird asymmetrical sleeves and dye it a nice wine color, but I'll wear it. Okay? So, have Andy call me, please! I don't mean to bug you, but as Lydia would say, Andy needs to speak now or forever take his seat.

I rode past SUNY Purchase and toward Purchase Street. I made a right and turned up Cottage Avenue and into the parking lot of the synagogue.

I jumped off my bike, threw it on the grass, and quickly whipped out my phone. I felt far too preoccupied to concentrate on my lesson or anything non-Andy related. I typed to Lydia fast.

OMG. Need advice.

I pressed send.
I waited.

Nothing.

I sent another.

> WYA???
>
> WYD??

Still no response.

> All g?

"Seema!" Rabbi Sherwin beamed as I entered the temple. "Come with me." He stuck his hand out behind him and I took it as we walked down the chapel aisle, past the rows of empty seats. It's funny how I didn't mind holding hands with Rabbi Sherwin or even having him call me by my Hebrew name, but when my mom or dad did either of those things, I wanted to straight die. "Today, we work from the bimah. *Bimah* is Hebrew for 'podium.' And you'll practice chanting your *haftarah*."

"You mean...we're going to sing?"

"Yes. Today we start singing."

"Um...Rabbi Sherwin?"

"Yes, Seema."

"I'm not a very good singer."

"Nonsense. I'm sure you're fine."

"I'm sure I'm not."

"Have you ever heard me sing?" he asked.

"No."

"Terrible," he said. "The worst. But this is not a contest. We sing because prayer is a celebration, a tribute." Rabbi Sherwin waved his hand toward the podium. As we approached, I looked out at all the empty seats and squelched a nervous giggle. The room felt very big, and I shivered a bit when I heard the echo of my giggle. I was aware of everything, it seemed. The presence of the cantor's lectern to my left, the holy ark for the Torah behind me.

Rabbi Sherwin handed me a printout with my Torah portion on it. "Hit it," he said.

I opened my mouth feeling really self-conscious. As if even the inanimate objects were watching me. The giant brass menorah with orange lightbulb candles to my left. The light shining through the Star of David on the window. The shofar on the table next to Rabbi

Sherwin. When I finally gathered up my courage to sing, all I could muster was some sort of muffled cross between singing and talking, the sound of answering a question when the dentist has their hands in your mouth. I was embarrassed for myself in front of myself. It was worse than the worst middle school audition. I peeked at Rabbi Sherwin, who looked slightly pained. I closed my eyes and opened my mouth and tried again. But the same sort of caterwauling came out of me. Then I tried a third time and a fourth, but I couldn't really get out anything more than a squeak.

The problem was obvious. I was having a creative block. I'd overheard my mom talking about this concept with friends, and it always sounded like she was describing procrastination. Now I understood—creative blocks and procrastination are not the same thing.

I couldn't get my brain to turn off and focus on anything other than if Andy Goldfarb liked me. It was as though my entire brain—creases, neurons, and whatever else Arthur knew about without having to look it up—had channeled all its energy into just one thing: Andy. If I spoke to him, I knew this feeling would disappear and I'd be able to relax and focus on equally pressing matters like singing my Torah portion. Not knowing was making me feel unbalanced, how I imagined Arthur felt all the time. I needed to clear my head. I needed to find out where I stood with Andy. Then, I thought, I would be able to sing.

I looked at Rabbi Sherwin and said, "I'm sorry, Rabbi Sherwin. I'm just having trouble today."

"Okay, then. Why don't you collect yourself, Seema. Go outside, get some fresh air, and meet me back here in five minutes."

Perfect, I thought.

Instead of walking outside, I ducked into Rabbi Sherwin's office and reached for my cell phone, only to realize I had left it at the podium! I looked around and set my eyes on the last living rotary phone in existence.

I quickly grabbed the phone and felt my heart hammering against my chest as I dialed Andy's long-memorized cell number. My palms were clammy and my stomach was backflipping and I felt far away and unreal as the phone started to ring. And ring. And ring. I hung up.

I looked at the photos on Rabbi Sherwin's desk of his wife and kids and all their millions of rescue animals. I took a long, deep breath and tried one more time.

The phone rang.

"Seeee-maaaah," Rabbi Sherwin called.

"I'll be right there," I yelled back.

"Seema! We only have fifteen more minutes! Where on earth are you hiding?" Rabbi Sherwin called.

"Rabbi, I'll be right there. I...I...I'm in the bathroom." On the third ring the phone was picked up, but no one said hello. All I could hear was a girl's shrill squeal and Andy saying, "Don't be punking me." There was another shriek, a giggle, some wrestling sounds, and then finally, a breathless girl, still laughing, said into the phone: "Andy Goldfarb's room." The voice was familiar. The girl went on, "Heeellllllooooooo?"

I didn't say anything. I knew this voice, but I couldn't place it.

"Speak now or forever take your seat."

I was stunned.

"Lydia?" I asked.

The door to the office opened.

"Stacy," Rabbi Sherwin started, "this is not the bathroom."

I was busted. There was nothing to do but hang up the phone. A tight lump in my Eve's apple (why should

Adam get all the credit?) started to form, and I could feel my eyes beginning to burn and water.

"I—I—" I stammered.

Rabbi Sherwin stood in the doorframe and looked at me, confused.

"I...I...needed to make a call," I managed.

"Who were you calling?" he asked.

"Um...I can't remember."

"You had to make a phone call, but you can't remember who it was you needed to call."

"Okay. I was calling...God?"

He looked at me strangely. Then he crossed his arms and took a very deep breath.

"Seema, what is going on here? First you tell me you are in the bathroom, but you are not in the bathroom, and then you tell me you had to make a phone call, but you can't remember who it was you had to call. This isn't adding up. Do you have something you want to tell me?"

"I—I—" I stammered again.

"Sit down, Seema. Why don't you tell me what's on your mind?"

"I have to go," I said as I moved out from behind his desk and past him. Then I shifted into a full-on sprint,

I heard Rabbi Sherwin call out from behind me, "Seema! We are not finished talking! Next time, we go fifteen extra minutes!"

I felt bad running out on Rabbi Sherwin like that. But I really had no choice. I just had to find out what Lydia was doing over at Andy Goldfarb's house.

7.
The Big Diss

*God, are you home? Is there something
going on I should know about? Because
I don't understand why you would
do this to me. Are you trying to teach
me some sort of lesson? Maybe one of
those valuable lessons they always tell
us about in Hebrew school? If so, I
have one request.*

*Please, please. Please, God. Please
don't make this be a valuable lesson*

*through hardship. I don't think I can
handle it.*

Okay.

Thanks.

I pulled into Andy's driveway and was near the house when I saw two people standing outside his front door on the grass. As I biked closer, I could see that one of the people was Andy. The other person was harder to see because Andy was standing in the way.

Andy and the other person weren't moving very much, which was strange. Like they were standing very, very still. I wondered why they were doing that and whether Lydia had already left his house. As I neared the edge of the driveway, I saw Andy hugging the person. I leaned the bike against the mailbox and started walking toward the house to get a better look. Suddenly I wished I hadn't looked. Because what I was seeing looked as if it was meant to be happening in a different world. A world in which only horrifying things occurred.

Andy Goldfarb, my beloved and recently un-renounced Andy Goldfarb, was kissing someone. And as he began to move out of the way a bit, I could see the someone better. I could see that the someone was wearing a shrunken corduroy blazer and high-waisted jeans. And that this someone had long brown hair. And stood like a dancer.

And that she was Lydia.

My heart stopped pounding, probably even beating, and the world around me grew very, very still. Tears climbed over their ledge and slid down my face, and as hard as I tried to keep them in, they just kept coming. I must have been making noise, because Lydia suddenly turned around.

"Stacy!" Lydia gasped. "I wasn't— We weren't—" She started and stopped. "It's not what it looks like."

Unless she was a cat grooming his face with her tongue, I was pretty sure it was exactly what it looked like.

"Of all people, I can't believe you would do something like this, Lydia Katz."

"You don't understand," Lydia said with teary eyes.

"What exactly am I missing? It looks pretty clear to me!" I yelled at her.

"No, you don't know. I can explain this, Stace, I really can."

"You are not a real friend."

Andy just stood there shuffling his feet back and forth like he was dribbling a soccer ball. Like this was the time for practice!

"Why would you do this to me?"

"Please, Stacy. I can explain," she pleaded.

I took a deep breath and counted to ten.

But by the time I got to three, I realized there was nothing to explain. My best friend, a girl who had never mentioned having a crush before, was a betrayer. Never mind the fact that I had publicly renounced my love for Andy.

At four, I was trying to calm myself again.

But by five, words were coming out of my mouth that never passed clearance in my head.

"Explain it to someone who cares, Lydia. Because I am not that person anymore."

I spun around and ran down Andy Goldfarb's driveway, taking off my friendship necklace and throwing it in the grass. But before I mounted my bike, it occurred to me that I had one last piece of unfinished business.

"Oh, and Lydia?" I started as I walked back up the driveway.

"Yes?" she asked hopefully, through her sniffles.

I braced myself for the hardest thing I have ever had to say in my entire life. And then as quickly as I could, I blurted it out, knowing full well it would forever change my most important friendship.

"Lydia, all I can say is that I hope you saved the sales receipt for your Stella McCartney dress, because you are SO not invited to my bat mitzvah."

8.

One Revenge and
Three Latkes

At dinner, my mother made potato pancakes in the shape of Hebrew letters. Just as she was handing me an aleph, my cell phone rang, and Arthur and I both looked to see Lydia's face fill the screen.

"It's Lydia," he said.

"I'm aware," I said.

"Aren't you going to get it?"

"No."

My mother looked at me and smiled. "Thank you for not answering your phone during dinner."

"That's not why I didn't answer it, but you're welcome."

My phone rang again, and again, Lydia's face filled the screen.

The next time it rang, Arthur asked, "May I?"

"Only if you tell her I moved to Abu Dhabi," I said.

"You want me to say that?" he asked.

"I don't care. Say whatever you want. I just don't want to talk to her."

Arthur looked around for a minute. The wheels in his head were churning. Finally, he grabbed my phone.

"Lydia, hi. This is Arthur Saul Friedman. I'm very sorry to inform you that due to a sudden onset of coma, Stacy has found herself infirm. We'll notify you if anything changes." He ended the call and looked at me, very proud of himself.

"Not bad, my boy, not bad at all," I said.

When my phone rang again five minutes later, Arthur looked at me, and when I shook my head, he answered again.

"Lydia, hi. This is Arthur Saul Friedman again. I have some complicated news to share. While we were eating dinner, some cloning experts for the human genome project 2.0 abducted Stacy to sequence and study her genetic code. Obviously, she's sequestered, but fear not, she'll be out and available to talk in thirty-seven years. If you know your future contact information, I'll have her get in touch in May 2052."

And at the end of dinner, while my mother was doing the dishes, the phone rang once again. This time, Arthur didn't even bother to look at me for permission.

"Lydia, hi. This is Arthur Saul Friedman. Things have taken a very unexpected turn. The Friedmans are so proud to tell you that Stacy just donated all of her skin to science. For the next ninety-four hours, she'll be sitting in the sun, drying out. We can't be certain she'll ever speak again, but miracles do happen. We'll know more once she's aerated."

Arthur had so much fun, he never even asked why I didn't want to talk to her.

And I have to admit, it warmed my heart to see him brimming with confidence for a change.

"Why I Want to Be a Bat Mitzvah" Speech

I want to be a bat mitzvah because I want to be an adult so I can slingshot myself out of Westchester and go live in New York City and be a famous stand-up comedian. Then I want to go on every late-night talk show and make the hosts laugh so hard that when they all retire, I'm the natural choice. After choosing whom to replace, I'll only book my friends as guests. Except for Lydia Katz, because in case you haven't heard, she's not my friend anymore. Even if she begs and pleads, there will still be no guest appearance. Andy Goldfarb, by this time, will have seen the error of his ways and made amends to me by taking a vow of fidelity. Each night, he will wait for me after taping and I will allow him to usher me home in a faux mink stole, while love-thief Lydia Katz is left friendless and alone, crying into the crusty toe pointes of her childhood ballet slippers, all because she betrayed me. And that's why I want to become a bat mitzvah.

9.
Mad Bothered

Kelly was pressed up against the mirror in the school bathroom, putting colorful rubber bands on her braces brackets. I was pacing the length of the bathroom, a practice I found to be quite soothing in times of stress. When she was done, Kelly laid paper towels on the sink, sat down, and stared at the stalls.

"You would think that the school would have put more thought into the color they use to paint their bathroom. Like, how is bright bile a good color?" Kelly asked.

Vandy, the school punk, was sitting cross-legged on the nasty tiled bathroom floor, holding a compact and cutting her hair into a faux-hawk.

"Can we get back on track, please?" I asked.

"Are you sure it was her? It just doesn't sound like anything that Lydia would do."

"You think I don't know Lydia well enough to know what she looks like when I'm yelling straight into all her face holes?"

"Well, it just seems so . . . out of the ordinary. I mean, I would have to say that out of the three of us, she is by far the nicest."

"That's what makes this all so strange."

"She's a swindler. That's what she is," Vandy offered from the floor. "A boy swindler, a scamp, a klepto-maniac, a rapscallion, and a con!"

We both looked at her, wondering if she even knew who Lydia was.

"Helpful. Thanks," I said, then turned back to Kelly. "Why would she do this to me?" I asked.

"It makes no sense. Especially since she doesn't even like boys," Kelly said just as Kym and this girl Jenn McKinley from eighth grade walked in.

"Who doesn't like boys?" Kym wanted to know.

"Lydia Katz," Kelly said.

"Who's Lydia Katz?" Jenn asked.

Kym turned to Jenn as if she was about to tell her everything. But then I saw her nudge Jenn's arm in a way that said: "I'll tell you later."

Jenn and Kym tossed their knapsacks next to Vandy and went into separate stalls. Kelly suddenly jumped down from the sink and stood in the center of my pacing path.

"Perhaps if we acted this out as an improv scene, we'd know what to do," Kelly said.

"Kelly, not everything is an acting exercise," I argued.

"You're not even willing to try. Come on. What would Kerry Washington do in a situation like this?"

The bell rang, and I headed toward the door.

"Kerry Washington would never *ever* be in this situation," I said.

"I guess you're right. The point is, I'm on your side, Stace," Kelly said, following behind me. It was taco day and the school hallway smelled strongly of beef. "I mean, I love Lydia as much as the next person, but this isn't just about party-crashing a crush. This is about loyalty," she added.

People were sitting in the hallway, in front of the lockers, AirPods in, listening to podcasts, copying each other's notes from class, and generally ignoring the fact that the bell had just rung. We rounded the corner and who should be walking right out of the science lab but Andy Goldfarb.

"Whaddup?" Andy asked me as he adjusted his G-Farb belt buckle.

"Nothing," I said as Kelly waved and kept on walking.

I hadn't seen Andy Goldfarb since I caught him kissing Lydia, and I was mad as hell. He took his Stüssy backpack off his shoulder and flung it on the ground near the lockers. He seemed blissfully unaware of my agony.

STACY FRIEDMAN'S STATEMENT REGARDING IMPA-TIENCE: Sometimes a person should dispense with the filler and actually get right to the point.

"How come you never called me?" I asked.

"Call you?"

"A few days ago, I ran into you at the Galleria and

you said you'd call me and we'd hang out, but then you didn't."

"Oh," he answered, and then started walking slowly toward class, leaving his backpack behind in the hallway on the ground. *Just how he did with my heart*, I thought. I followed him, waiting for a better response.

Oh? That's it? But then he opened his mouth, which gave me hope that he was going to make things right again.

"My bad."

My bad, meaning he was sorry? *My bad*, meaning he wished he'd never kissed Lydia? *My bad*, meaning he loves me instead? *My bad*, meaning he doesn't know why he did what he did, but he can explain it and take it all back?

"Word. Did you get the four-one-one on Aaron Barowitz's soccer bar mitzvah? It's mad cool. Kid ain't even good at soccer. But check this, yesterday—"

"Are you going out with Lydia?" I cut in.

"Huh? What? Lydia? Lydia Katz?"

No, Lydia Bennett in *Pride and Prejudice*.

"Yes. Lydia Katz."

"I dunno." His face suddenly flashed a deep red. And then, "What'd she say?"

"I don't know," I answered. "We don't speak anymore."

"No cap? That's mad weird; I thought you guys were like tight. Did something happen?"

I stared at him, incredulous.

"We had a fight. I un-invited her to my bat mitzvah, remember?"

"Oh, yeah. That's right. Whaddya do that for anyway?" he asked.

And then it dawned on me. He had no idea that I loved him. Only Kelly and Lydia knew. And the Pipers, of course. "It's a long story," I said, suddenly embarrassed at maybe giving myself away. "Anyway, I'm late for history."

And then, as if the run-in with Andy weren't stressful enough, I turned and ran head-on straight into Lydia. I was rushing down the stairs to class and she was slowly meandering up. My stomach pleated with nerves when I saw her. My plan was to pass her without a single word. Maybe just a glare or an annoyed groan or something. But she ruined my plan by speaking first.

"Stacy, I don't understand why you're so mad at me."

I was dumbstruck.

WHAT?!?!

WHY?

WAS?

I?

SO?

MAD?

AT?

HER?

Had she broken her head?

"How could you not know?" I asked her, perplexed.

"I don't know, I just don't," she said, looking like she was about to burst into tears. She always seemed to know what I was thinking or feeling, but on this one she was just numb or something. I wanted to shake some sense into her. I wanted to say, "You stole my crush, my dream man, my future husband and bat mitzvah date!" But my pride wouldn't let me. Besides, there were too many people around to hear.

"You don't know much, Lydia Katz. Do you?" I said.

I left her, climbing the stairs two at a time. I had

never stayed angry at her for this long in my entire life. Not speaking to her felt really weird. And it would probably get even weirder. Like, for example, at Kym's sleepover this weekend.

How could Lydia and I be at the same sleepover and not speak? That would be like Hailey Bieber and Selena Gomez showing up at the Teen Choice Awards and not fighting.

10.
Mitzvah Madness

The day of my next bat mitzvah lesson, my mother told me that instead of dropping me off at the temple, she'd be coming inside with me. When we got there, Rabbi Sherwin was waiting for us on the outside steps. I ran ahead of my mother as soon as I saw him.

"How are you feeling today, Seema?" he asked me.

"Good, Rabbi," I said, looking at the ground.

"I called your mother last night and asked her to stay so we could all speak about what happened the other day."

I looked at him, horrified. And if my mother knew about this, why didn't she say something about it to me? The car door slammed, and I heard the high-pitched tones of the automatic lock. Then the click-clack of my mother's high-heeled shoes making their way toward us.

"What do you mean? What happened?"

"You were making a call from my office without permission, and you lied to me." I was stunned silent. I couldn't believe that on top of all my other problems, I was about to be in trouble with my mother because I was in trouble *with my rabbi*!

"Please please please leave my mother out of this, Rabbi Sherwin. I'll explain everything to you, but please. I'm begging you. Don't tell my mother." Rabbi's right eye started to twitch a little, which happened sometimes when he was thinking. He pursed his lips a couple of times and looked up to the sky. I hoped he was thinking quickly. My mother was almost within earshot.

"Hello, Rabbi," she called as she walked up the steps of the synagogue.

I looked at Rabbi Sherwin, who took my mother's hand in his.

"You look lovely as always, Shelly," he said.

My mother blushed and laughed. "Thank you, Rabbi," she said.

"So, " my mother said. "What's this all about?"

Rabbi looked at me and I looked at the ground, embarrassed.

"Well, I thought I would just report quickly on Stacy's progress," Rabbi Sherwin said to my mother, gently touching my shoulder. "She's doing very well," he said as he looked at me.

"I'm thrilled to hear that," my mother responded.

"There's just one small thing..." Rabbi Sherwin continued.

WHAT? What was he doing to me?

"What is it?" my mother asked, concerned.

"If you don't make enough kugel for me to bring home to Mrs. Sherwin next time, I'm going to get in very big trouble."

I breathed a huge sigh of relief. My mother, looking relieved herself, laughed and said, "I will keep that in mind."

When my mother walked back to her car, I turned to Rabbi Sherwin.

"Thank you," I said.

He opened the synagogue doors, and we stepped in. I followed him toward the bimah, but halfway there he stopped and slid into a pew. He motioned for me to slide in next to him and I did.

"So? Tell me what's going on," he said.

I shook my head, but it didn't fool Rabbi Sherwin because tears started to fall. I was so embarrassed. Who cries in front of their rabbi?

"I don't think anything will help," I said through my tears.

"Try me," he said.

I wiped my tears with the back of my sleeve.

"Life is just so unfair," I cried. "You know Lydia Katz, right?" I asked him.

He nodded.

"And you know she's my best friend, right?"

Here he nodded again.

"Well, she's not my best friend anymore. In fact, she's my sworn mortal enemy."

"Go on," he said gently.

"Okay, here goes. Lydia Katz kissed the boy I love. Not only did she know that I loved this specific boy, but this specific boy said he'd call me and then he didn't and claims he doesn't even remember saying he would call me and today at school I saw Lydia, who I'm not even talking to, and she doesn't even understand why I'm mad at her!"

Rabbi Sherwin shook his head. "That's a lot of bad news."

"I know. I don't know what to do. I wanted to have a boyfriend by my bat mitzvah, so I'd have someone to dance with, but also because it's the first day of my adult life, and if that day isn't special, then maybe my entire adult life won't be special either. And now, not only do I not have a boyfriend, I don't even have a best friend!"

"That's a lot of disappointment."

"So, what am I supposed to do?"

Rabbi Sherwin rose and I rose too. He started toward the stage and I followed him. Maybe he had a book of answers hidden behind the ark. But he stopped halfway there, in between the pews, and looked up toward the stained glass. The sun was leaking through in long diamonds and casting a warm, bright light on his face. He turned to me and spoke slowly and deliberately, as if delivering a message he had just received from God.

Gee, thanks, God. You make time for
Rabbi Sherwin and not me? What do I
have to do to get your attention? Go to
rabbinical school?

"It seems as if everyone else has the things that you want, doesn't it?" he said as he continued to the stage. I slid into a pew and he talked as though giving me my own private sermon.

"Yes, it does," I said, thankful that someone finally understood me.

"And you don't want these people to have what it is that you wanted. What's yours is yours, and what's theirs is theirs. Is that correct?"

"Yes!"

Was Rabbi Sherwin God dressed in man's clothes? How did the man know all this about me?

"I think that the only way a person can be happy is to want happiness for others. That's called righteousness. The path toward righteousness begins with acts of loving kindness. When a person performs acts of loving kindness, they do so munificently, without expecting any recompense. The actions become the reward.

With each deed, he is fomenting a connection with God."

I wasn't sure I was following. For one thing, Rabbi Sherwin was using words I didn't understand. *Recompense? Munificently? Fomenting?* I did, however, understand one word.

"Rewards?"

"Yes, by performing service to God and acting out of loving kindness without expecting anything in return, a person reaps untold rewards."

This was sounding awfully familiar.

"You mean like doing mitzvahs."

"Yes, exactly," Rabbi Sherwin said, looking down at me from the stage.

I didn't think he knew what he was talking about. *What good is a mitzvah going to do*, I wondered. It wasn't going to change what Lydia did. It wasn't going to help me get Andy. No, revenge was better. Maybe Rabbi Sherwin was an expert on rabbi-related matters, but I was an expert on seventh-grade-girl-related matters.

"I find that it's helpful for students of the Torah to learn about their portion before singing it to the congregation. Since your Torah portion is about sacrifice, I think now would be a marvelous time for you to start thinking of ways you can give of yourself or *make sacrifices* for others.

"You, Stacy Adelaide Friedman, are hereby advised to perform three mitzvot before your bat mitzvah."

"Three?"

"Three. It is time for you to put a face on the project. Let's put God on your guest list, shall we? Trust me, when you do for others, the rewards are exponential."

There he was, going on again in rabbi code. I think he was hinting at the fact that if I did my three mitzvahs, chances were strong that I'd be rewarded with Andy Goldfarb's love. This was brilliant. Instead of being evil to get even, I would get even by doing good. Who could resist that? Three mitzvahs. That wasn't so hard. I just had to pick three people to do things for. Three people in a few weeks and then Andy Goldfarb would be mine.

Rabbi Sherwin opened my bat mitzvah folder.

"Shall we begin?" he asked.

Yes, I thought. We shall.

11.

Sacrifice Is Not a Four-Letter Word

I walked home the long way from my lesson, contemplating all that Rabbi Sherwin said. I had to figure out who would be on the receiving end of my mitzvahs and I had to do it quickly if I was going to have them done in time for the bat mitzvah. But when I got to the sculpture garden in between the temple and my house, I was momentarily called away from my mitzvah planning by shouts in the distance.

As I neared the source of the shouts, I saw some

older kids from school piling on some poor kid. I wondered if this was the kind of thing that would start happening to Arthur if he didn't work on his coordination. I had started to veer away a bit when I heard my name.

"STACY! STACY!"

I looked around but didn't see anyone.

"STACY! OVER HERE!"

I turned and saw two long limbs waving and writhing from under a pile of boys.

It was Arthur!

"HELP ME!" he screamed.

I ran toward the pile, yelling at the kids to get off of my brother. One by one they climbed off Arthur and scurried away as I ran toward them. I reached out my hand to help him up, but I wasn't strong enough. Finally he got on all fours and stood up slowly. His nose was bleeding and he was shaking and out of breath.

"Are you okay, Arthur?" I asked.

"Used to it," he answered.

"You are?" I asked, completely surprised.

"Yeah, they usually leave my face alone. That's how

they can get away with it. If they don't leave visible marks, there's no obvious evidence."

I put my arm around him. I knew that kids made fun of him for being so smart, but I didn't realize they were physically hurting him. It broke my heart.

"Did you try running away from them?" I asked.

"I'm a brain, Stacy, not a jock."

I never really bothered to think about how hard it must be for Arthur. Mostly because I was too busy thinking about myself. But also because if I'm thinking about him at all, it's usually about how much he annoys me. "Come on, Arthur. Let's go home," I said.

We walked in silence past the pond, down the hill, and on Lincoln Avenue toward home. Cars passed on both sides of us, and I wondered whether Arthur and I would ever get out of the holes that were dug for us. After all, Arthur was bigger than all those boys combined, and they still managed to clobber him. But then I realized, if people smaller than Arthur could hurt him, then people smaller than Arthur could help him! Or in plain English with a pinch of Hebrew, he could be my first mitzvah! I could help him get more coordinated and outrun those boys. Or fight back, if he had to. Then those boys wouldn't pick on him! It was perfect! And what a happy coincidence that I happened to be walking through the sculpture garden right after my talk with Rabbi Sherwin.

I looked up at Arthur, who looked down at me with grateful eyes. Yes, this was right. *Arthur Saul Friedman, I secretly anoint you my first mitzvah.*

When we got home that afternoon, my mother was waiting for me with a pile of books and what looked like a small gift box.

"These are all books on sacrifice. I thought you'd like to look through them to get some ideas for your bat mitzvah speech."

I took them from her.

"And this is from Lydia. She stopped by earlier and wanted to give you this." She handed me the gift box.

"Thanks, I guess," I said.

"Did something happen between you two?"

I groaned. "No—God, Mom. You're so annoying. Nothing happened. Everything's fine."

"You don't have to speak to me that way, young lady," she snapped.

"Sorry," I said, and then added, "Is that all?"

"Yes, Stacy. That's all," my mother responded, hurt.

I shut my bedroom door. Why was I being so mean? It wasn't her fault that Lydia was a traitor.

I looked at the gift box for a minute before shaking it. It rattled and I slowly unwrapped it. The box was from Rags to Riches, our favorite store, now long gone, but inside the box was something of mine. It was my half of our friendship necklace that I had torn off and thrown at the adulterous feet of Katz and Goldfarb. There was a note. It read: *I'm so confused and I want to make up. Will you please talk to me?*

This was big. Lydia was seeing the error of her ways. I wanted to forgive her so badly.

But how could I? She had crushed my Andy Goldfarb–shaped dreams.

Then again: She'd been my best friend since we were practically bald.

Maybe at Kym's sleepover tomorrow night, she and

I could figure things out. And after she apologized and I forgave her, maybe she would just hand Andy Gold-farb over to me!

End of story.

Then I wouldn't even need to perform the mitzvahs anymore.

Right?

12.
Dream a Little Dream

Dear God,

    I had the BEST dream last night. I was at my bat mitzvah, at the bimah, and at the end of my speech, everyone got out of their seats and gave me a standing ovation. Suddenly, Andy Goldfarb walked down the aisle in a tuxedo and I realized that I was not at my bat mitzvah, but MY WEDDING!

When I looked down, I was wearing
the gold pleated dress that I got stuck
in (only this time I wasn't stuck, and
it fit perfectly) and I knew without
even looking that I had to be at least
40 percent prettier. Then he got to the
altar and we exchanged vows and I
looked over at Lydia, who was standing
next to her boyfriend, who was NOT
Andy Goldfarb. And it was just perfect.
Please, God, let this be a secret message
you're sending me.

While I packed for Kym's sleepover, I thought about how cool Lydia was for making the first move. Now all she needed to do was find herself a great new boyfriend. Then once Andy and I were married and Lydia and her new boyfriend were married, we'd live together in the same loft building in Manhattan. Probably Tribeca. We would have dinner parties together, see art on Fridays, and shop Bleecker Street on Saturdays, and when we had children, we'd stroll our babies down Fifth Avenue together, have picnics in Central Park, and dress up for

Lydia's premiere in *The Nutcracker* at Lincoln Center. We'd all live happily ever after.

As I opened my dresser and started pulling out clothes, my bedroom door flew open, and Arthur stood there in his ridiculous and far-too-short-for-him SpongeBob pajamas. His face was glistening with that same excitement he had when he'd just cracked some advanced NASA code, or whatever he spent time doing in his brain. He was shoving a bagel with cream cheese so quickly into his mouth, he almost choked. It was true, he did eat too fast. Maybe that's why he was growing so fast. He needed to slow down. After he finished coughing, he stood there staring at me while cream cheese stuck on the end of his nose like a skin flap. Then he started hiccupping.

"What are you staring at?" I asked.

"The space-time (*hiccup*) continuum," he said.

"What do you want, Arthur?" I asked.

"Is Sara Langley (*hiccup*) going to be at Kym Armstrong's party?"

"Yeah. Why?"

"Then I'm going in the car with you. Don't (*hiccup*) leave without me. I'll go change."

Arthur ran out of my room and into his. Sara Langley? She was almost thirteen and he was, well, *ten* and, well, not remotely cool enough for a Piper. Who was he kidding? I was about to go into his room and ask him what made him think a girl *days* away from puberty would go for a boy *years* away from puberty, but then I remembered that he was one of my mitzvahs and as such, it was my job to help him, not taunt him. I quickly ran downstairs, cut open a pomegranate, split it into quarters how my mom showed me, then put them in a dish and set them outside his bedroom. There was literally no way for anyone, even Arthur, to eat a pomegranate quickly. Then I ran back into my room and began packing.

I fished out an old knapsack from the back of my closet.

Then I opened my hamper, where I keep my two secret, totally un-Mrs.-Shelly-Friedman-authorized outfits, and shoveled one of them into the bag. I zipped up and was about to carry the bag downstairs when I realized I couldn't possibly go to a slumber party without a backup outfit. I returned to the hamper, lifted the wicker top, pulled out a stash of hidden makeup, and shoved in a couple more outfits. From my closet I pulled out a few pairs of pants and a few of my dad's perfectly worn-in college sweatshirts. The space in the knapsack was getting smaller by the minute. I pulled down a bigger bag, but after putting everything in there, I remembered that I hadn't even looked through my drawers yet and there were bound to be T-shirts and tights and things I'd want to bring also. I mean, what if I only brought jeans and shirts, but everyone else was wearing skirts and boots? Or what if everyone was wearing a nightgown and I just had my pajamas? I didn't want to stand out, especially not in front of the Pipers. I mean, this was sort of our big initiation. So I went to the hallway closet and lugged out the biggest suitcase I could find. By the time I was done packing, I had nearly every piece of clothing I'd ever bought or borrowed or had handed down. This was the first real slumber party with the Pipers—a girl had to be prepared with any and all outfits.

Just as I was trying to move my suitcase, Arthur came barging into my room. "Hey!" he yelled, dangling his sock in my face. It was drenched in what looked like watered-down blood.

"Get your nasty bleeding fungus away from me," I yelled, scooting quickly to the other side of the room.

"Why'd you put a pomegranate outside my door?"

"So you'd eat it," I said.

"Well, I STEPPED IN IT!" he yelled at me, and then stormed away, red sock in hand. Oh, boy. He was going to take much more work than I thought.

I went outside, where I was going to lie out for twenty minutes to get a base tan before getting the real tan at Kym's. I saw my mother a few hundred yards away by the compost bin, talking to someone who looked exactly like my father. As I got closer, I realized it *was* my father. He'd never come to visit before unless he was picking up Arthur or me. I wondered what he was saying to my mom. Maybe he was getting rid of that awful Delilah and was now trying to get back together with my mother. Just like she had hoped for!

I had started to run down the hill toward them when they both turned. I yelled, "Daddy!" I almost jumped into his arms, but then I caught the expression on his face.

"What's the matter?" I asked.

"Nothing, baby. I'm just talking with your mom."

"But why do you guys look like something bad happened?"

"No, sweetie, nothing bad has happened," my mother said. "I'm just tired. Daddy's leaving now anyway."

"You're not staying, Daddy?" I asked.

"No, sweet pea, I have to go, but I'll see you soon."

He was leaving. My mom looked miserable, and he looked pretty unhappy himself. I realized I was off base. It was pretty obvious that whatever he came to say had nothing to do with dumping Delilah and getting back together with my mom. I felt so bad for her. And for me. But mostly for her. It just didn't seem fair.

I guess life really just isn't fair sometimes. Which feels very...

Unfair.

13.

Goldfarbmania

My mom drove Arthur and me to Kym's house. On the way, I opened the box from Rags to Riches. Lydia had decorated it herself with words that exclaimed *Forgiveness! Friendship! Forever!* I took out the friendship necklace and slipped it over my head. And then I rubbed my half of the charm for good luck. My half had the word *best*; Lydia's side said *friends*.

"Did you know that Sara Langley is already thinking about colleges?" Arthur asked.

Nobody answered.

I looked over at my mother, who was being very quiet.

"Mom?" I asked.

"Hmmm?" she said.

"I love you," I said softly.

"Oh, sweetie. Thank you. I love you too," she said.

"Hey! What about me?" Arthur called from the back seat.

"What about you?" I said, teasing.

"Stacy!" my mom scolded.

"Just kidding." Then, "Yeah, you too, Arthur. I love you too."

"Did you know that Sara Langley is planning on taking AP Physics in ninth grade?" Arthur asked.

When we pulled up to Kym's house, my mom and I got out of the car. Arthur got his arms caught in the seat belt trying to unbuckle it. I swear there was no one more uncoordinated than that boy. I helped him free his arms just as Kym and Sara Langley ran up to greet us. Sara made Arthur so nervous, he caught his foot in the seat belt strap and fell, face-first, out of the car and onto the gravel. Kym and Sara stifled their laughs as my mom helped Arthur up. Arthur stood there, dumbfounded. Pebbles and gravel stuck to one side of his face. Poor kid.

"Hi, Sara," Arthur said a little too loudly and with parts of the pavement still attached to his cheek.

"Hi, Artie," Sara responded, brushing her cheek off as a message to Arthur to brush off his own. A message he didn't pick up on.

"Actually, it's just Arthur. Not Artie. Or Art, for that matter. I mean, I like art as a discipline—particularly abstract expressionism—which is neither here nor there, but not as a name."

I gently shook my head at him and then Kym grabbed my hand and the three of us skipped away down toward the pool. I screamed goodbye to my mom and Arthur, and as we disappeared down the grassy path toward the pool house, the two of them climbed back into the car.

Lots of girls were there already, sunbathing in their bikinis. Kelly was slathered in baby oil and was squeezing lemon in her hair. When she saw me, she got up and ran over. The other girls followed. Everyone started talking to me at once.

"We totally heard what happened between Andy and Lydia, you must so totally hate her," Megan said.

I had never felt so popular before. I never knew that all it took was some drama to get a group of people to circle around.

"I heard Lydia and Andy did it in the water at the quarry. What a slut. We think it's disgusting. Don't we, girls?" Kym said. All the girls nodded in agreement. I played with my friendship necklace.

"Thanks, guys. I really appreciate that," I said, feeling slightly guilty. After all, we were about to make up and be best friends again.

"I heard from Lila who heard from Marcus who heard it from that punk girl, what's her name? Vampy?" Kym said.

"Vandy," said Megan.

"Right. I heard that Trampy said that Lydia Katz was just using Andy as a decoy because she's really in love with YOU."

All these rumor-y things they were saying about Lydia were beginning to make me uncomfortable.

"I don't want to spread lies about Lydia. Plus, we're

probably going to make up today, so let's stop the meanness, okay?"

The Pipers nodded in agreement, but I could tell they were disappointed. They wanted to be catty.

Another car pulled up, and soon Lydia was walking our way. Everyone turned around and saw her and before her face even came into focus, they all left me and ran over to her. Only Kelly stuck around. I was stunned. I thought we were all in it together!

"This whole situation has turned into a very dramatic and compelling scene. I wonder how Kerry Washington would play this," she said.

When they had gathered all the information they needed from Lydia, they headed back toward me and Kelly. It felt like some weird showdown, like in the old Westerns that my father used to watch. Lydia trailed behind them. Kym pushed her toward me, and as she stood in front of me, everyone quieted down and waited to see what would happen, who would draw her weapon first.

"Hi, Stacy," she said to me.

"Hi, Lydia," I said back.

"Guess we should talk," she said.

"Yeah. I guess so," I responded.

I was so excited to have her back in my life. I had entire days of things to tell her. And then as soon as Andy was mine, we could get to work on finding her a boyfriend. Then we could talk about our boyfriends together and there would be no jealousy. The idea of this made forgiving her betrayal so much easier.

"Stacy, listen, I—" But before she could finish her sentence, we heard the distinct sound of a boy commotion. I looked toward the grassy patch and there, on their bikes, were Andy Goldfarb, Dante Decosimo, and Rob Mancuso riding right toward us.

Seriously, God? You really had to send them over, now?

The boys were whooping and hollering, and when they got to us, they braked and skidded off to the side.

"How's the party going, girls?" Rob said.

"Fine," Kelly answered, eyes wide like she had seen Kerry Washington do. "How'd you know we were here?"

"Kym told us to come by," he said.

I kind of wished Kym had told them to come by just

a little later. By that time, Andy would have been fair game.

There was a pause while people figured out what to say next. Andy broke the tension. "Damn, you ladies got me bent—y'all looking criminal."

Everyone sort of squirmed with elation. As far as we could tell, making a boy feel bent and looking criminal were definitely a plus. We were all quiet and then one by one people started to look at Lydia and then at me and then at Andy and there was this weird force field that I didn't know what to do with. I guess Lydia didn't know what to do either, because both of us just stood there.

But then Andy looked over at Lydia and smiled and winked, and when he did that, Lydia walked over to him, put her arm around his waist, and kissed him right on his mouth.

Um, God?

What kind of apology was that? I swear, people let out gasps. Andy seemed startled and he pulled away and then sort of swatted at his lips to wipe off the offending saliva.

Kelly grabbed my arm and said loudly, "Come on,

Stacy. We have better things to do than watch Mrs. Betty Betrayalstein." And we walked off toward the chairs to get ourselves some sun.

I was devastated. That was so not how it was supposed to go. What happened to the best friend reunion tour? How could she give me back my friendship necklace and then one day later throw it back in my face by kissing MY ANDY GOLDFARB in front of all these people? In front of me? I was THIS CLOSE to googling whether or not friend duplicity was illegal. Why wasn't there a place to press non-literal charges against people who hurt you emotionally? If that place existed, I'd stand on that line and I'd wait all day long.

God! I'd like a word, please....

14.
Avocado Schmear with a Side Order of Fried Friendship

It was becoming a party divided.

After the infamous kiss, we retreated to the kitchen, where we scoured the refrigerator for ingredients. Avocados, mayonnaise, olive oil, bananas, Crisco oil—anything fit for a spatula. We were going to make food masks. I started with some honey on Kelly's face and then layered on some oatmeal. Megan was busy mixing sugar, water, and canola oil because she heard that was an excellent exfoliant.

Honestly, I would have preferred being in my bed curled up in the fetal position crying myself to sleep, but I took Lydia's lead and pretended I didn't care about her or Andy or whatever it was people were saying they did at the swimming quarry. It was so strange—one minute we were about to make up with each other, the next we were icing each other out.

But truth be told, I cared so much, I feared I might never recover if I let myself feel even an ounce of this hurt. So, in the spirit of trying not to care, I stayed.

A huge island counter divided Kym Armstrong's kitchen in half. Kelly and I and these two girls that I never knew anyone was friends with, Lucy Trellis and Amanda Stern, were stationed on one side of the table, and Lydia, Kym, Sara Langley, and Megan were seated on the other. I guess no one, especially not the Pipers, loves a loser.

Soon Lydia's side of the table began whispering and gossiping and we tried our hardest to ignore them. It felt as if Lydia was now confirming every bad thing I ever thought about myself. Like even though she used to tell me that I was beautiful and amazing, she must not have ever really meant it. If she had, then why would she have done this?

As Kelly rubbed avocado on my face, I was starting to feel vaguely claustrophobic. She mixed some Crisco with banana and castor oil and dropped a handful on top of my head before kneading it in. Then Megan Riley said, "So Lydia, is Andy a good kisser?" a little too loudly for my taste.

Lydia whispered her answer and all the girls started giggling.

Lucy Trellis turned to me and said, "You're too good for Andy, Stacy."

And then on Lydia's side, Megan said, "Stacy couldn't get Andy if she tried."

And then on my side, Amanda said, "Yeah, well, Lydia clearly deserves a boy who breaks up a best friendship. Stacy does not."

And then Kym gave the ultimate hit.

"Maybe Stacy couldn't get Andy because she thinks she's funnier than she actually is."

And that just did it. I was furious. I got out of my seat, ran my fingers across my eyelids to clear off the avocado gunk, and walked over to Kym, shaking and fuming. I stuck my finger in her face and said, "You know what, Kym? You're about as funny as my Torah portion—which is about sacrifice! Also, it's very interesting to me that all of you are overlooking a very vital fact."

Everyone looked at me.

"Andy wiped Lydia's kiss off his lips. He didn't even want her dumb saliva anywhere near him. Am I the only one who noticed that?" I yelled.

"He did not," Lydia said, defiant, but then scrunched her eyebrows as if perplexed.

Kelly chimed in, "I noticed it."

Lydia crumpled her nose as if she smelled a school of dead mice.

As Megan pondered the statement I had just made, Sara Langley licked Nutella off a wooden spoon.

"See! What do you make of that, huh, Kym? How serious could he even be about her?" I shouted.

"Not everyone likes public displays of affection. Not everyone needs to be the center of attention, Stacy. You ever think of that? Besides, we all know that you're just jealous because he chose Lydia over you. You couldn't have gotten him if you tried. Oh wait, you did try!" Kym yelled back.

She was the one who started this whole thing. She was the one who suggested I could get him in the first place. They all agreed I should be the first one to have a boyfriend, and now they were saying I couldn't have even gotten one if I tried? I was furious. And then when Megan giggled and Sara looked over at her and smiled knowingly, I blew another fuse.

"You know what, Kym? You and Lydia can sit home reading the dictionary the day of my bat mitzvah for all I care, because you're not invited either!"

"Well, then you're not invited to mine," Kym countered as two cucumber peels slid down her face.

"Yours? You're not even Jewish. Yours is a goy mitzvah!"

Then I whipped around to Megan, who, underneath a mask of mayonnaise, had a devilish smirk on her face that declared she was definitely not on my side, and I said, "You gonna be number three? Huh?"

Something in me had snapped. I couldn't contain myself. I turned to Sara, who rolled her eyes at me as she coated Kym's hair with margarine.

"You want out too, Sara? You wanna be uninvited? Because I'll do it. You just say the word, and you're out."

I was prepared to tell Arthur to find a new crush, that Sara wasn't worth it after all, but she didn't say anything because clearly she wanted to come to my bat mitzvah, but then Kym blurted, "Stacy, in case you haven't noticed, everyone's had it with bat mitzvahs. There's too many. The last thing this world needs is one more bat mitzvah!"

"Good," I yelled, throwing a spatula on the floor. "BECAUSE YOU ARE NOT WELCOME! You and Lydia can stay home together bored out of your heads while everyone else is at the best party they've ever been to in their entire lives!"

"We don't care!" Kym yelled back.

Oh, she better care.

"I don't care that you don't care!" I yelled. "And you know what else? Anyone who cares as much about other people's personal lives as you do clearly has no inner life!"

I turned around and started to leave, but then I spun back, whipped off my friendship necklace, and threw it at Lydia's feet, and felt momentarily pained when I saw it had bent. Then I stormed out of the room, ran upstairs, called my mom, lugged my suitcase downstairs, and waited on the front lawn for my mother as avocado hardened on my face.

15.
What's the Matter Is
What's the Matter!

I really missed my dad. If he still lived at home, he'd have been lying on his bed, watching one of his surgery shows. Not realizing that Kym's party was meant to be a sleepover and that something must be wrong because I'd left early, he'd ask me how it went. I'd pretend it went well and everything was fine—because what do fathers know about betraying friends and boys and kissing anyway?—and in some small way everything *would* be fine because sometimes it felt good to have someone be kind of clueless and at least he was there to ask about it.

But now all I had was Arthur.

"Why'd you come home?" he asked, jumping on the bed and grabbing the DVD remote. Of course Arthur was aware it was supposed to be a sleepover.

"Because girls are stupid," I said.

"That is inaccurate," he answered.

"But then again so are boys."

"Also inaccurate."

"Honestly, maybe all people are just hopelessly disappointing."

"Probably more accurate, but generalized statements are instantly defaulted under the umbrella category known by one and all as inaccurate."

"Arthur, will you please stop saying that?"

"It is under consideration," he said, flipping to an old episode of *Nova*. "Did you really come home because of Lydia and Mr. Cultural Appropriation?"

"Oh my God, seriously? He's just cool. Get over it."

"Inaccurate. Ignorance is not cool. Cool is knowing

better. If you'd like some unbidden advice, mine is: Pay closer attention."

"Whatever, Arthur," I said, grabbing back the remote. "Do you know why Daddy was here before?" I asked, changing the subject.

"No," he answered. Neither of us said anything for a minute. I felt as if I should say something, being the older sister and all, but it wasn't Arthur who needed comforting.

"You shouldn't watch so much TV, Arthur. Why don't you do something more athletic?"

"It's nine o'clock at night. What do you want me to do?"

Good point.

"How about some mindful eating?"

"Do you want me to eat the pomegranate seeds off my sock now?"

"Oh, forget it," I said.

I walked out of my parents' room. Correction, I walked out of my mother's room.

In my bathroom I scrubbed the leftover dried avocado from my face with a loofah. My mother came into the bathroom and sat on the edge of the tub.

"Stacy, will you please tell me what's the matter?" she said.

"I already told you in the car. Nothing!" I snapped.

"Well, something must be the matter," my mother answered, annoyed. She stood and started hanging up the towels that were on the floor. I grabbed one of them out of her hand and dried off my face.

STACY FRIEDMAN'S STATEMENT OF FACT CONCERN-ING MOTHERS TRYING TO GET THEIR DAUGHTERS TO TALK TO THEM: If you're a mother and you want your daughter to talk to you, do not keep asking her, *What's the matter? What's the matter? What's the matter?*

"Is it about Lydia?"

"No, Mom."

"Is it about a boy?"

"No, it's nothing. Please. You're so annoying. I don't want to talk to you. I don't want to talk to anyone!"

And then my mother's eyes misted over, like she was about to cry, and she turned her back on me and said in a quavering voice, "Fine, Stacy. Don't talk to me."

And she stormed out.

Oy.

I sat down on the edge of the tub and pulled at the

loofah. If my father were here, he'd know what to do. He'd leave me alone. If Lydia and I were friends, she'd do something now to make me laugh.

I couldn't sleep. I was imagining Kym's party and all the bad things everyone must be saying about me. I hoped so hard that they wouldn't turn Kelly against me. She was my last remaining friend. I was also feeling horrible about making my mother cry. She didn't mean to be so annoying. She was having a hard time just how I was having a hard time. It's just that my hard time felt a little more pressing than hers. Or, more accurately (sorry, Arthur! I guess I do see the value of accuracy!), I just didn't know how to go about fixing anything.

What's more—I still had to get going on the mitz-vahs! So far, I'd only found one and it wasn't going very well, as evidenced by Arthur's little display with Sara Langley this morning. Not to mention his continued disinterest in learning to be more coordinated and less clumsy. I also felt guilty about thinking I was off the hook with the mitzvahs. I hoped God hadn't heard me.

I wondered if Lydia felt as bad as I did or if she just

didn't care about me at all anymore. I was afraid I'd have to get new friends. I certainly wasn't going to be part of the Pipers now. And I could also forget about the Crew since they were all connected. I was going to have to be friends with people whose opinions I disagreed with, like Marni Gross.

I tried very hard to turn my brain off. Just as I was starting to float away toward a dream, I smelled something strange and musty, and I woke up.

Was that smoke?

I pushed the sheets and blankets off me and went to investigate. It didn't smell like a fire; it smelled like something else. And it was coming from the kitchen. I quietly crept downstairs and through the living room. I opened the swinging kitchen door, and I heard a slight shifting noise. There before me was the startling sight of my own mother, Mrs. Shelly Friedman, smoking a cigarette!

A *cigarette*!

My mother didn't even drink Manischewitz wine.

"Stacy! What are you doing up at this hour?" She tried hiding the cigarette behind her back, but the smoke was curling toward the ceiling.

"I couldn't sleep."

I pulled a chair out and sat next to her at the table. I didn't know what the cigarette meant, but it meant something. Was she losing her mind? A nervous breakdown? Did she have a secret life as a French intellectual and I was just now catching on?

"I didn't know you smoked," I blurted.

"I don't, really," she insisted.

"Inaccurate," I said, gesturing to the lit cigarette in her hand.

"I used to. Before I was pregnant with you. But I quit. I have a cigarette about once a year, maybe even less."

"Why?" I asked.

"Well, sometimes it makes me feel better even though in the end it always makes me feel worse."

My shoulders slumped, remembering when I called her annoying in the bathroom.

"I'm sorry I made you cry," I said.

"Oh, sweetie. You didn't make me cry. I was already upset. It had nothing to do with you."

Relief washed over me, even though I felt bad that

she was upset about something else. *It wasn't my fault, God, see?*

"Then why?"

"There is something I need to tell you. I was going to tell you in a couple of days, but I might as well just tell you now. It's not a big deal at all. But your father came by today to tell me that he plans to bring Delilah to your bat mitzvah."

I figured I must have heard her wrong.

"What?" I asked, bewildered. "Delilah?"

"Delilah," she said.

I stared straight ahead, unable to meet her eyes. We sat side by side like that for a while, just staring silently out at the kitchen. Was my dad serious about this person? Did this mean that the separation was now going to turn into a *divorce*? And how was it that the people I *did* want to be at my bat mitzvah were so not invited and the people I *didn't* want to be there were now invited? This made no sense.

"But then who are you going to go with?" I asked.

"Well, I guess I'll have to go alone," she said.

Alone? That would be awful for her.

No, this was not right. She could not go to my bat mitzvah alone.

My mother tamped out her cigarette and rinsed the ashtray.

"Don't tell Arthur I was smoking," my mother said.

"I won't," I promised. She kissed the top of my head, wished me a good night, and went to her bedroom.

I opened the refrigerator and took out some leftover dinner. While I ate ratatouille straight out of the container, I wondered how I could help my mother.

And then it occurred to me. It was so simple. I don't know why I hadn't thought of it before!

My mother would be my second mitzvah. If my father was going to bring his maybe-not-so-new girl-friend, then I would have to find someone for my mother to bring. There was no way I would let her go to my bat mitzvah alone.

That settled it. All I had to do was find my mother a man.

16.
Dress-Tastic!

"Why I Want to Be a Bat Mitzvah" Speech (Attempt #2)

I want to be a bat mitzvah so that when I make other people cry, I will be adult enough to know how to make things better.

I want to be a bat mitzvah so that I can make adult decisions and say adult things and be taken seriously. Like, for instance, I would like to say to my mother that instead of wearing her baggy clothes and her hair pushed back in one of those dumb plastic headbands, she should get all decked out and use my bat mitzvah as an opportunity to wow my dad so that he'll feel dumb for choosing someone as plastic as Delilah over her. And I would also like to say to my dad that I know that I give Mom a hard time about a lot of things, but she really is very thoughtful, and considerate, much more so than Delilah, who was the one who pushed for meeting us when we didn't even know she existed. My mom is classy and sweet and cares about everyone even if they don't deserve it. And he will never find a better woman than my mom and doesn't he even want to spend time with his own family again?

God, I don't know how to do this. A bat mitzvah speech is too hard to write. Who can write these well? Not me, that's who can't. I can't do anything right. I'm stuck. Please unstick me.

More soon.

P.S. I miss Lydia.

I shoved my second-attempt speech into my bat mitzvah folder. I started wondering about extreme makeovers and whether there was enough time to sign my mother up for one of those shows. Maybe we could even get on one of those shows where they pay for an entire new wardrobe for her. And while onstage, I could show the audience the god-awful dress my mother was planning to make me wear and have them scream and hoot and jeer so much at the outrageous ugliness that the host would buy me a new dress.

I opened my closet door, got down on all fours, tossed out some shoes, and scurried around back there until I found the offending dress. I needed to double-check and see if it was gross enough to get me on television.

Just then my door flew open. I spun around, startled.

"HOLY brain hemorrhage, Batman. It's that *thing* again." Arthur walked in and jumped up on my bed.

"What thing?"

"That thing you had on the day Delilah came over."

I rolled my eyes.

"Did Sara Langley say anything about me?" he asked.

At the mention of Sara Langley, my stomach rollercoastered. I didn't want to think about any of the Pipers right now.

"Like what?"

"I don't know. Whatever it is girls say about boys that they like."

"She doesn't like you, Arthur."

"That is inaccurate."

I turned around and looked at the dress again.

"You're not seriously going to wear that, are you?" he asked me.

"What choice do I have?"

"Plenty. You could 'lose' it; you could find a stain on it that you must have 'overlooked' before. You could develop a sudden allergy to it."

I turned to face him. How did he come up with these ideas?

"What else?" I asked, interested.

"Plenty," he said. He lay down on my bed, crossed

his arms behind his head, and shut his eyes. "You want my help?" he asked.

"Yes," I said reluctantly.

"And what will you do for me?" he said.

I thought for a minute.

"I'll talk to Sara Langley about you," I said, without even the tiniest clue as to how I'd make that work, since we weren't even speaking.

He bolted upright.

"You will?" he asked, grinning.

I nodded.

"Follow me," he said, leading me to the laundry room.

He loaded the dress into the washer, poured a combination of liquid and powdered soap into the machine, set the washer to hot, and pressed start. We watched an episode of *The Simpsons* and then threw the dress in the dryer. An hour later, the dress was the size of a Cabbage Patch Cutie outfit.

Holy wow. My brother *was* a genius.

17.
Absolutely Nots

- Nothing above the knee
- No black
- Nothing low-cut
- No spaghetti straps
- Nothing strapless
- Nothing that can pass as lingerie
- Nothing that requires you to wear a thong
- No metallic
- No mesh

- Nothing from any store that could pass
  for a nightclub
- Nothing sheer
- No chains
- No metal studs
- No fast fashion
- Nothing over $220

And so went the list. After seeing the shrunken dress, my mother did not do any of the following:

- Scream
- Yell
- Get red-faced
- Call my father
- Go berserk
- Punish me

Instead, she looked up from the scarf she was knitting, gently asked what happened to the dress, and wrote the above list. Her calmness worried me. It wasn't like her to be calm. It was as if she had no fight left.

I felt terrible for her. I wanted to make her feel

better. I wanted to tell her that she didn't have to give up, because I was going to fix the Delilah disaster by finding her a date. But I couldn't just yet. I didn't want to raise any false hopes.

"Call a Lyft and take Arthur with you to the mall," my mother said, still seated on her new knitting rocking chair. "Arthur, you're in charge of the list."

Arthur reached for the list as I stood there, shocked at how well Project New Dress had gone.

In the Lyft I called Kelly to make sure the Pipers hadn't turned her against me after I left the party. She told me they didn't. They all watched *Real Housewives of Dubai* and dehydrated random condiments in a dog treat jerky maker.

"Great," I said. "Wanna meet me at the mall?"

Turns out she was already there.

I hung up the phone and leaned against the back seat, staring out the window as we quickly passed cars and trees. Arthur and I were quiet, confused.

"I've never seen Mom like this before," I said.

Arthur didn't say anything. He just kept staring out the window.

"Have you?"

Arthur still didn't say anything.

"Arthur, we have to help her. We have to get her a nice Jewish boyfriend to bring to my bat mitzvah."

"It's time to Shellybrate," he said.

"Excuse me?" I asked.

"It's time to Shellybrate," he repeated.

"What are you talking about, Arthur?"

"That will be Mom's profile name when we sign her up on JDate."

"JDate? How do you know about JDate?"

"I happened across it as I was researching for chance and probability class."

The kid was off his rocker.

"What's that got to do with JDate?"

"I am afraid the explanation will be over your head. Suffice it to say I was searching online and a pop-up ad for JDate came up. That's how we'll find her a boyfriend."

"On JDate?" I asked.

"That is accurate," Arthur answered.

The cab stopped and let us out in front of the Galleria. Arthur lumbered out of the cab, and as we walked to the lobby to meet Kelly, I asked Arthur how he proposed we'd get on mom's laptop to do this without getting caught.

"Young Stacy, you have so much to learn," he said, adding, "The UPS Store is at the Galleria, is it not?"

Okay, this boy had gifts. I smiled broadly at him, and we went, list of absolutely nots in hand, to meet Kelly.

Too-Tall-for-His-Age Boy Genius was going to help Average-to-Above-Average Cute Girl perform her second mitzvah.

18.

Queeny Jerk & Her New Best Friend

Inside the Galleria, the old couples power walked through the corridors like they were at the gym instead of the mall. Kelly and I liked to tease each other about which outfit and fanny pack we'd be wearing at that age.

We passed Bath & Body Works, Famous Footwear, LensCrafters, and Holy Guacamole. We decided to head over to Macy's, the safest bet. Hopefully I'd find something conservative enough to satisfy my mother but short enough to make me look at least slightly fashionable. As we passed Cinnabon and rounded the corner, we heard some kids calling out: "Go, Dante, go, Dante, go, go, go, Dante."

There was a substantial crowd. Maybe two or three rows thick. Kelly, Arthur, and I looked in and saw Dante wearing an Oculus Quest headset. He was doing the most amazing dance moves I'd ever seen. I scouted the crowd and saw Andy Goldfarb, Sara Langley, and Megan Riley. No Julie Haven. No Kym Armstrong, and most important, no Lydia Katz. Maybe the mall banned them all for bad behavior.

After seeing who was and wasn't there, we decided to go in and made our way through the crowd. Arthur watched Dante with such intensity and such longing.

"Do you think that someone taught him how to be cool or he arrived at it naturally?" Arthur asked me.

"I don't know. Can cool be taught?"

"Yes, I believe it can. Maybe Dante has a Udemy class."

I looked back at Dante and wondered if he could be the answer to Arthur's problems. Not that I thought cool could be taught. But if Arthur took dance lessons from Dante, he'd probably learn some coordination. Maybe he'd finally sync up with his out-of-proportion body, which, let's face it, would bring him one step closer to cool, but more importantly would keep him from getting beaten up and picked on. I wished I could ask Dante for his help. But it seemed like a stretch.

I guess I hadn't studied the crowd well enough, because a couple feet behind and to the left of Andy and Rob stood Lydia Katz and Kym Armstrong, arm in arm. My stomach sank. Oh, so now Lydia was best friends with the Queeny Jerk? Was I that easy to replace?

Jealousy filled every last one of my pores. And the jealousy increased as I realized that all the Pipers and all the Crew were there at the same time.

And Lydia was not just with Kym. She was with all of them.

Did that mean they all came together as a group and Kelly and I weren't invited? Just then, Kym noticed me in the crowd and with a smirk pushed Lydia toward Andy. I nudged Kelly.

Andy's back was to Lydia and she scooted so that she was next to him. He didn't seem to notice and Lydia turned back to Kym, who jutted her chin out as if to say, *Just do it!* Then Lydia put her arm around his shoulders.

But as soon as he felt the touch, he turned toward Lydia and shrugged it off.

Um, God? What was that?

Lydia's face turned that strange rash red that meant she was embarrassed, and then Kym whispered something in her ear and Lydia shook her head and whispered something back. Then Kym got this bossy look on her face, and Lydia leaned over to Andy, whispered something in his ear, and then...

SHE WENT IN FOR A KISS!

Right there in the mall in front of everyone. In front of me!

And then the worst thing happened. Or the best, depending on whose side you were on. He ignored her kiss; he turned his head away from her as she went toward his lips and just kept on watching Dante with his hands in his pockets.

It was awful.

It was humiliating.

It was exactly what I would have wished for if you had asked me five minutes earlier.

It was the ultimate blow, and somehow, I don't

know why, I felt bad for Lydia in that moment. Maybe because I knew how bad it felt to be snubbed.

Why was Lydia acting this way? It was like she was ignoring all the signs he was sending her and behaving the way she wanted him to behave. Even I could see that. And I barely knew one thing about boys.

It was then that Lydia happened to spot me in the crowd. I guess I didn't want to make her feel worse, so I averted my gaze, pretending to be fully engrossed in Dante's performance.

"Did you see that!?" I practically shrieked at Kelly once we made it inside Macy's.

"See what?"

"Lydia! Andy!"

"No, I missed it."

"How could you have missed that? She went to kiss him, and he totally blew her off! Where were you?"

"I don't know. I was having audition fantasies."

"Kelly. What you just told me is punishable by law. You missed the most monumentally awful thing ever. I will now replay it back to you, vertebra by vertebra."

Over racks of dresses, I told Kelly the entire melodrama while Arthur looked through racks to get ideas for our mom's new style.

Almost the second I finished recounting every last detail of the now presumably infamous Goldfarb Galleria blow-off, Lydia and Kym walked into the store. Kym saw us first and she immediately went in another direction. Lydia kind of hovered near us, probably trying to eavesdrop.

Poor Lydia.

I walked over to her. Kelly kind of hung back and didn't meet Lydia's eyes. Because she had just been so publicly hurt, I felt as if I should make the first move. I had a heart, after all.

"I'm sorry things didn't work out with you and Andy," I said.

"What do you mean?" she countered haughtily.

"Oh, I— Uh…" She wanted me to make her relive the moment? "I saw what happened, when he—"

"Oh, that? We're together," she said. "He just doesn't like public displays of affection."

I nearly Shakespearean-died! I wanted to scream, *I*

was just being NICE, since you obviously just made a FOOL of yourself!

Kym walked over to our rack, hooked her arm into Lydia's, and said, "Yeah. They're together!"

I couldn't think of what to say. I mean, obviously Andy had blown her off. Or was it obvious? Maybe I was confused? But then why did she hover near me at the store? Was she trying to reconcile? Apparently not.

A few minutes later they walked out of the store and Kym turned to Lydia and said loudly so I could hear, "We are SO not friends with them."

It was true. And I SO wished it weren't.

I was pretty bummed out. I would have gladly, at that moment, worn the shrunken dress to my own bat mitzvah if it meant not having to live my life fighting with Lydia. Don't get me wrong. I loved Kelly. She was so supportive of me, but she didn't know the first thing about depressed moms with obsessive knitting disorder or genius brothers with limbs growing faster than they should disorder. But Lydia did. Her mom was also moody and, well, she didn't have a brother, but I'm sure she'd know what to do about Arthur. Lydia was the one who always made me laugh, or at least made me feel better about things.

But I couldn't think about that now. That Lydia was gone, I guess.

When we went to collect Arthur from the "New in Designer Fashion" area, he wasn't there. I panicked. Kelly and I roamed the mall, stopping in every place that sold books or science things, but there was no Arthur.

We went back to Dante's dance circle, thinking he might be watching, but everyone had left. I was about to page him from the information booth when Kelly spotted him coming out of the UPS Store, looking exhilarated and panicked.

"Where've you been?" he asked, flailing his arms at us as if we were the ones who'd disappeared on him.

"Arthur, you never even told us that you'd be here," I said, stating what should have been the obvious.

"Never mind that, what does Mom look like?" he asked.

"What do you mean, what does she look like?" He wasn't making sense. It was beginning to scare me.

"I need help describing her for her JDate profile."
He grabbed my hand and dragged me into the store.
Then he led me to a desk with a computer on it. There
was an ad on the screen and Arthur was jabbing his finger at a section titled "About Me." It was an ad for...
our mom?

"It's missing something," he said.

I took a look at it.

Single in Westchester, with completely
average twelve-year-old daughter and
code-cracking, ten-year-old prodigy son
who will one day change the world, but for
now is satisfied with simply making his
family proud, seeks kind man with whom to
share Shabbat dinners, possible more. I like
gardening, knitting, and speaking Hebrew.

"What a rip-off," I said, quickly replacing *completely*
average with *comedically gifted* to my description.

Arthur shook his head. "Stacy, please focus. We're trying to find a mate for our mother. Not you. Studies have

shown that men seek certain physical traits in potential female partners. Shouldn't this be addressed somewhere?"

He was right. His description lacked a certain je ne sais quoi. I deleted it and started over.

> Beautiful young Westchester divorcée,
> mother of two, seeks someone to enjoy life
> with. I am independent, intuitive, a good
> listener, and I do Yogalates every day. I have
> traveled six continents, shaken hands with
> two presidents, and had my poetry published
> in several journals. I'm looking for the right
> man to escort me to my daughter's bat
> mitzvah. Perhaps that man is you.

"How does this work for you?" I asked.

He gave it a quick once-over. "Is that stuff true?"

"Probably as true as anything anyone else wrote in their profile."

"That is accurate," he said, clicking on the publish icon.

So, the ad was posted. Which was great because I needed to get back to my shopping.

Well, God, we finally found something.

It's a one-shoulder tulle dress in dusty pink. It has a zipper back and a cute satin belt, and it comes with a matching clutch! Arthur compared the outfit to the list of absolutely nots and I compared it to the original vision I had of myself on my big day. Although she didn't say no to one-shoulder, I know my mom will be a bit upset, but when you find a loophole that works in your favor and doesn't hurt anyone, you have to use it, right? It falls a little short of my ultimate dream dress, but I never did own a purse before.

So, that's something.

Now, if we could just nail my three mitzvahs, I'd super appreciate it!

19.
Time to Shellybrate!

Mom was in the kitchen, sorting through the bat mitzvah RSVPs.

"We got an outfit," I said, excited.

"That's good," she said, not looking up.

I looked at Arthur. She was still acting strange.

"I'm hungry," Arthur said.

"The refrigerator is right behind you, Arthur. You can make yourself something."

Arthur looked at me and curled his eyebrows, displeased.

"Uh, that's okay. I'll wait until dinner, then," he said, and raced away to his science lab to work on the most current model of his brain.

I stood there swinging the shopping bag back and forth, looking at my mom, who was busy opening envelopes and ticking off names on a piece of paper.

"You okay, Mom?" I asked.

"Fine, Stacy," she said. And then added, "Why?"

"I don't know. You seem... like you're not in a good mood."

"I'm in a fine mood," she said. She didn't sound fine to me. She sounded worn down.

"Do you want to see my outfit?" I asked, hopeful.

"Maybe later."

"Oh," I said, disappointed.

I couldn't wait to read the messages on JDate and then tell my mother about her prospects. Maybe seeing how popular she was, that she was still desirable, would lift her spirits and put her in a better mood. We could bond like we used to when I was younger. I could put makeup on her and curl her hair. Maybe she'd even want to go shopping for a new, more updated style and take me along with her. Maybe I'd even tell her what was happening with Lydia and Andy. It was getting too hard to hold it all in.

But when I opened my mouth to say something more, she just closed her eyes, like the world was making her very, very tired. Maybe even too tired to mom.

God, should I be worried?

20.
I'm Bad, I'm Bad,
You Know It

Two nights later, my mother left us with about three thousand emergency phone numbers and went to a meeting at the Women's Hebrew Society. As soon as she left, Arthur and I ran to the TV room (which was also the office, reading room, and dining room when our mother wasn't home) and logged on to JDate to see if there were any messages.

There were eight.

The problem was how to judge the degree of grossness. I mean, anyone the age of a parent is pretty much romantically disgusting. Arthur read the responses and the descriptions of the men out loud while I paced and eyed an episode of *Riverdale*. We narrowed it down to two people: Ross Geller and Judge Dreidel.

Arthur began to get hungry while he ticked off a list of Ross versus Dreidel pros and cons. I decided to try one last time to get him to eat a more mindful and healthy diet. At the very least, he would definitely feel better, which would give him more confidence to stand up to his bullies. I left him alone to battle out the personals.

I pulled all the vegetables and fruits out of their crisper drawers. I dragged the blender out from the cabinet underneath. Then I cut up and loaded in beets, carrots, celery, peppers, kale, an orange, a kiwi, and two pears, and blended it all up. Then I chopped up some tofu and put it on top of lettuce and in between two pieces of bread. "Arthur!" I screamed at the top of my vocal cords. "Dinner!"

He came running down the hall as if responding to some native call. He slid into his chair and before I could even catch his reaction, my mother came in through the front door.

"What are you doing home already?" I asked.

"I didn't feel like being there. Everyone was talking about their husbands this and their husbands that. I just had to leave."

She dropped her bag on the couch, took her jacket off, hung it up, and headed toward the stairs.

"I have a terrible headache. I'm going to lie down." In the kitchen both the shake and Arthur were gone, but the sandwich was untouched. I heard strange retching noises from the bathroom and went in to find Arthur throwing up in the toilet.

"Are you trying to assassinate me?" he yelled, and then stuck his head back down the toilet. When he brought his head up, he said, "Is this some sort of psychological experiment you're brokering?"

"It's good for you!" I defended.

"Good for me? Since when is death good for me?"

"STACY!" my mother yelled from upstairs.

Ugh. What gives?

"Don't go anywhere," I said to him.

I ran toward my mother as Arthur yelled out, "Very funny!"

My mother was lying on her bed with all the lights out. One arm was strewn over her eyes.

"Are you okay, Mom?" I asked, concerned.

"Stacy, could you please wet a washcloth for my head?"

"Sure."

I went in the bathroom, ran a washcloth under the faucet, squeezed out the excess water, and brought it back to my mother, who placed it on her forehead.

"Thanks, sweetheart. Did you and Arthur eat?"

I wasn't sure how to answer that.

"We're in the process," I responded. "Mom, are you okay? You are freaking me out."

"Just a headache. I'm sure I'll be fine after I rest."

I shut my mother's door and ran back down the stairs. I was beginning to worry about her. She was a mess. Arthur was apparently feeling better, because he was standing at the foot of the staircase, holding his shirt in one hand.

"I vomited on my shirt," he said as he tried to hand it to me.

I backed away.

"Arthur, I am not touching your puke."

"Why not? You made this exact puke in the blender."

He did have a point.

"I'm unmoved," I said.

"What's the matter with Mom?" he asked. "I want a real dinner."

"She has a headache, and besides, you just puked. Give your system a minute to reset."

Arthur rolled his eyes.

"You're such a bad sister," he said to me, and walked away. I stood in the front hall for a little while. Was that true? Was I a bad sister? A bad daughter? Was I even a bad friend? I was trying so hard to make good mitzvahs, but all of my efforts were either backfiring or going unnoticed.

I was beginning to wonder if it was time to give up.

21.
Lessons in Coordination, Italian Style

That night, after Arthur went to bed and my mother was fast asleep on top of her sheets and still in her clothes, I called Kelly. I was telling her about the JDate finalists when I was hit with a bit of Arthur's genius. Arthur was enjoying helping me out with our mom. Maybe Dante would enjoy helping me out with Arthur. People liked it when other people wanted their help.

I quickly hung up with Kelly. I ran downstairs to the kitchen, took my class list down from the bulletin board, and picked up the phone, but then immediately hung it up. You can't just make a phone call of this nature without being prepared. One did not just call a gorgeous Italian guy on a whim. My palms were suddenly very sweaty, and I was annoyed at myself—anything boy-related always made me so nervous. I dialed. It rang once and I almost hung up. It rang twice and I almost threw up. On the third ring a voice said, "Hallo?"

"Um...yes. Hallo. I mean, *hello*. Is, ummm... Dante Decosimo there, please?"

"Yes. Is Dante."

"Oh. Okay, then. I didn't know. Hi, Dante. This is Stacy Friedman, from your class?"

"I know who is Stacy Friedman. Tell me."

"Ummm...okay. Well, it's kind of a long story, but my little brother, Arthur, used to be really small, like four foot nine, but over the past year he's had a crazy growth spurt and now he's five foot seven—at least today. Tomorrow, who knows? Anyway, this acceler-ated growth spurt hasn't given him enough time to learn how to coordinate his limbs, so he loses his foot-ing all the time; he trips, or hits people by accident. He has no sense of his body in space and because of that some kids at school have been bullying him.

"I'm supposed to do three good things for people before my bat mitzvah and since you're such a great dancer and so coordinated in general, I was wondering if you'd maybe help Arthur so that he'll be able to run away from the kids who are always chasing him and beating him up?"

Why did I just tell him every single detail of everything that's ever happened in this house? Did I mention I still hadn't gotten my period and that I found a stray hair on my nipple and was slightly convinced I might possibly be turning into a different species right before everyone's eyes?

"I do it."

Wait, what?

Did he say he'd do it?

I never thought he'd actually do it. How lucky am I?

"Thank you! When can you start?"

"As soon, if it is possible."

"What about the day after tomorrow?"

"Day after tomorrow, she is good. Arthur, he is lucky to have very nice sister like you."

"Oh, no. I'm not a nice sister. You've got the wrong girl, Dante."

"This is Stacy Friedman, yes?"

"Yes, Dante." How could he not know who he was talking to?

"Then I know she is the right girl," he said.

For some reason, what Dante said just then gave me a little lump in my Eve's apple. Which was strange because I wasn't even sure what he meant. Which was also strange because usually I had no trouble understanding him even though everyone else did. Suddenly I felt the need to hang up the phone.

"Okay, Dante, see you the day after tomorrow."

I couldn't believe it. The mitzvahs were finally getting off the ground. People were responding to the online ads, Dante was going to help Arthur get coordinated and maybe even learn how to dance, and it would all be because of me. How could I not be rewarded for all that? How could Andy Goldfarb not see all the good things I've done for other people and fall madly in love with me?

And finally, how could I find a third mitzvah, let alone get it done in time for my bat mitzvah?

22.
Another One Bites the Dust

The following night, Arthur and I were seated alone at the dinner table. My mother wasn't hungry and had opted out of dinner in favor of curling up in her knitting chair. And the huge salad I made was sitting untouched.

"I've decided on Ross Geller," he announced, pummeling fistfuls of Cocoa Puffs into his mouth.

"Arthur, are you sure you wouldn't rather have some nice ready-made tofu ravioli for dinner? I could pop it in the microwave."

He vehemently shook his head and then said, "Can you stay focused here, Stacy?"

"Okay. Ross Geller. But why?" I asked.

"He doesn't have kids. The other one has a nine-year-old daughter and the last thing we need in this house is a stepsister," he answered, his mouth filled with crispy brown morsels.

"Good point."

Arthur ate in silence. Then, "There's one hitch," he confessed. "The only time he could do it was tonight."

"Do what?" I asked.

"Go on a date."

"Are you kidding me? It's for tonight?"

"Well, yes. That's the only time this week he could arrange it."

"Well, Arthur, it already is tonight."

"Well, Stacy, I realize that. That's why I'm telling you. So you can tell Mom."

"Me?!"

"Accurate."

"No. Not accurate. And didn't it ever occur to you that Mom would need more than a few hours to prepare for the date? I mean, not just to get showered and changed, but also to get used to the idea of dating again?"

"No," he said. He might be a genius at everything else, but he was comically clueless when it came to dating and social situations.

"Why do I have to tell her?" I asked.

"Because you're older," he argued. "And because you're both girls. And also, because he'll be here in about two hours." Arthur got up to clear his unused plate and utensils.

Well, that was accurate.

I sat alone at the table for a few minutes. I was really concerned about my mother. She hadn't stopped knitting since skipping out on the Women's Hebrew Society meeting. Seriously, if she kept it up, we would probably have to add an extension to the house just to make room for the scarf. She could probably just knit the extension herself.

I cleared my place and headed upstairs to deliver the news. She was, of course, in her knitting chair.

"Mom, you really need to eat something," I said as I plopped myself down on the edge of her bed.

You also might think about changing your clothes,
and showering, I thought but didn't say.

"Not hungry," she managed.

> *What's happening here, God? I thought*
> *this was supposed to be the happiest*
> *time in my life, but it's the worst.*
> *Arthur can't stop eating and my mother*
> *won't eat a thing. Andy is nowhere near*
> *close to being my boyfriend. Lydia and*
> *Kym are best friends, and no one seems*
> *to like me anymore. And the fact that*
> *I'm in danger of not coming up with*
> *a third mitzvah means that things are*
> *potentially only going to get worse.*

"How about I make you some spaghetti?" I offered,
since spaghetti was the only thing I knew how to make.
Other than salad.

She shook her head.

"Mom, Arthur and I have a surprise for you."

She looked up expectantly.

I took a breath. Now or never.

"We made a profile for you on JDate," I said proudly.

She kept a steady eye on me, not blinking or moving her head.

"Mom?" I asked. "Did you hear me?"

Her face was absolutely blank.

"Take it down," she said.

What?

I was stunned.

"Delete it."

"Why?" I asked.

"I never asked you to do that, Stacy. You have crossed a boundary."

"But Arthur has already arranged for one of them, Ross Geller, to pick you up in two hours and take you out."

At this my mother looked at me.

"From *Friends*?"

Huh? Was she forgetting the names of her friends?

"No, we don't know him."

She put her knitting needles down.

"Call him and cancel."

"We don't have his number. It was all arranged through e-mail."

"Well, get online and tell that poor man not to come."

"Mom! Please, just give it a chance. He looked really great."

"Stacy, please don't push back on this. I'm not going to budge," she said, picking up her knitting needles and continuing with a scarf so long, it would make the Torah scroll blush.

What can I say, God, Arthur and I tried everything.

We messaged the guy. Then we messaged him again, but it was too late. He wasn't logged on. We sat and stared at the computer, refreshing JDate every few minutes to see if he got our message not to come. But he didn't. I took up pacing. Arthur started tapping his fingers on the desk. He fiddled with some paper clips and began wiring together a model brain. He tried refreshing the computer one more time. Suddenly the doorbell rang, and startled, I screamed. Which in turn made Arthur scream.

We both ran to the door.

"Charlie Weinstock," a respectable-looking man said as he stuck out his hand to shake mine.

I stared at him. Who was Charlie Weinstock?

He banged his hand to his head. "My bad," he said, sticking out his hand again. "Ross Geller."

Oh!

"Hi, Ross," I said, not knowing how a person could get his own name wrong. Other than that not-so-small detail, he was actually not bad-looking. Not bad at all. Maybe Mom would change her mind after she saw him.

"I'm here for TimeToShellybrate," he said. "You must be the bat mitzvah girl."

Arthur led him into the living room and proceeded to entertain him with questions that would stump most Mensa members. I ran upstairs. My mother was exactly as I had left her.

"Who was at the door?" she asked without looking up.

"Ross Geller."

"How did I fail to make myself perfectly clear?" she asked.

"We tried, Mom, we really tried, but we couldn't get to him in time. He seems really nice. Very gentlemanly.

Good manners. Really good. Extremely handsome."
This got her to look up. But instead of asking interested
questions, like "Did he look you in the eye when he
shook your hand," she just said, "Please tell him to go
away."

"But, Mom..." I started.

"No buts, Stacy. Tell that gentlemanly, good-
mannered man to go away."

"Really, Mom. You should at least look at him.
Even I think he's cute, and you know I'm very judgmen-
tal. Please? For me?" I begged.

She looked down at her project and continued to
knit and purl while I stood there staring at her, waiting
for an answer. Finally, she said quietly, "Stacy, I'm so
tired of fighting. Please just send that poor man home."

I turned around slowly and headed back down the
stairs. Arthur was lecturing Ross on intellectual prop-
erty law in the living room, and when he caught my
eye, I slowly shook my head. Arthur stopped his lecture midstream, which must have seemed a little fishy
to poor Ross Geller.

"We apologize. Our mother has suddenly fallen
immediately ill. Too sick for socializing. She tried to

reach you online, but apparently you didn't get the note," Arthur said.

He shifted his weight awkwardly. Then he shrugged, looking me in the eye. I glanced away. "Well, if she changes her mi—I mean, when she feels better, ask her to e-mail me. We can reschedule."

As we watched him disappear in his car, I turned to Arthur.

"So much for that idea," I said, disheartened. Now my second mitzvah was a total wash. God was going to be so pissed.

23.
Dante as a Second Language

Dante and I biked over to my house together after school, and strangely enough, our conversation wasn't strained. And unlike the other day, I understood everything he said.

Who knew I had such an ear for second languages? Much less Italian? If only I could decipher Andy-speak as well as I could Dante-speak.

We had time for ice cream, so we stopped and ate our cones on a bench.

"In Italy there isn't this planning for everything.

You just do what you want without stress. We take time without rushing. Here everyone goes fast to the mall and then fast to their McDonald's."

"But still, in Westchester, life is much slower compared to the city," I said. "The Big Apple," I added.

"The Big Apple," he repeated. Then, "*Mela*."

"*Mela*?" I asked.

"Apple," he said.

"Oh! *Mela*," I repeated.

"*Bene*!" he said.

Cones inhaled, we hopped back on our bikes and headed to my house.

Arthur was home already, in his room, wearing headphones and watching a Udemy class on aerospace engineering. I went and closed the laptop on him.

"Hey, what gives?" he asked, removing his headphones.

"I have a secret to tell you," I said.

"What?" he asked.

"Sara Langley told me something."

"She did? Is it about me?" Arthur asked, suddenly red-faced and sweaty.

"Yes," I answered.

"Well, what is it?" he demanded.

"That she'd like you on one condition."

"What's the condition?"

"That you learn how to control your limbs with more grace and aplomb so you stop accidentally smacking people and knocking everything over," I said.

Of course, Sara Langley still didn't know Arthur existed. But that was beside the point.

STACY FRIEDMAN'S STATEMENT ON LYING: Sometimes it's okay to lie if it's for a greater good.

"Well, how am I gonna do that?" he whined.

And then I held out my arm toward Dante, who was standing in the doorway, and said, "Meet your personal trainer slash dance coach."

Arthur took one look at Dante, awed that someone so cool was actually in his room, extended his shaking hand, and said simply, "This is accurate."

24.
Katz vs. Goldfarb

During lunch hour, Kelly and I stole away to the library to write my bat mitzvah speech. She looked at what I had so far, which was pretty much forty variations on nothing.

"Stacy, this is awful."

"Well, fix it."

Kelly got up and went into the stacks, pulled out a bunch of books with quotations, and plunked them all down on the desk.

Sometimes we played a game with our class list

where you close your eyes and whoever's name your finger lands on is the boy you're going to end up with. We decided this was the best approach for picking quotes for my bat mitzvah speech. She flipped randomly to a page, and I shut my eyes and laid my finger down. I opened my eyes and saw that I chose "How is the Empire?" attributed to George V.

"Who is George Vee?" she asked.

"George the Fifth, dummy," I said.

"Well, who is he?"

"No idea."

We tried again. "It is as healthy to enjoy sentiment as to enjoy jam."

Okay, another, then.

"Between two stools one sits on the ground."

"Wow, who wrote these?" Kelly asked. "Maybe you should just start off with something that will make people think you're deep and sensitive."

"I stand here before you today a woman?" I offered.

"Perfect!" Kelly said as she grabbed the books to return them to the shelves. I was sitting thinking of my next line when suddenly I heard Kelly shout-whispering for me.

"What?" I shout-whispered back.

"Come here!" she responded, frantically motioning for me to join her in the stacks.

Kelly pulled some books off the shelf as she urgently waved her hand for me to join her. Then she made a little window so we could eavesdrop. And wouldn't you know it. It was Andy and Lydia. And they were fighting. Lydia was leaning against the wall and Andy was kind of pacing.

"Why do you go everywhere I go?" he asked, kind of mean.

"Because you're my boyfriend," she said.

"But I'm not your boyfriend. We had a pact, remember? But now you're like all up in my face!"

Lydia didn't say anything. She just looked at the ground.

"Why can't we just be cool?" he asked.

"I don't know," she answered.

"So, stick with the pact. A'ight?"

She didn't look up. She just nodded. And then he turned around and walked out of the library, leaving Lydia alone.

A pact? She had a pact with Andy? What kind of pact?

I was so confused.

Kelly turned to me and whispered, "He's yours."

Lydia leaned back against the wall and started to cry. First it was a light cry, but then it grew progressively heavier. When her shoulders started bobbing up and down, I knew she was really feeling it. Part of me wanted to go to her and tell her that it was all right and that what he said was mean. But then I remembered that what she had done to me was mean too. Especially now that I knew there was some sort of pact.

Even if I was confused about what that pact might be.

But before I could decide if I wanted to go comfort Lydia, I realized something else: Andy Goldfarb was available. He was free. I still had a chance. I could still be the first one in our class to have a real boyfriend. I couldn't believe it.

Plus, the timing was perfect.

Now I wasn't just the Stacy Friedman he'd known since grade school. Now I was the Stacy Friedman who did all these nice things for people. I was Stacy

Friedman with the extra boost of mitzvah confidence. Stacy Friedman with a little extra glowup. And that Stacy Friedman was completely irresistible.

Unless that Stacy Friedman didn't find a third mitzvah, in which case she could be back to square one.

25.
The Andy Goldfarb Chapter

Stacy
&
Andrew

Stacy Adelaide Friedman, the daughter of Shelly Fried-
man and Dr. Morton Friedman of Purchase, New York,
is to be married today to Andrew Joshua Goldfarb,
son of Mitzi Goldfarb and Lenny Goldfarb, also of
Purchase, New York. Rabbi Sherwin is to perform the
ceremony at congregation Emanu-El of Westchester.

Coincidentally, they will be getting married at the same temple where young Stacy Friedman became a bat mitzvah, the same day that Andy Goldfarb kissed her for the first time and professed his undying ever-lasting forever love.

The bride, almost thirteen, is in the seventh grade at the Rye Country Day School in Rye, New York, where she excels in American literature but needs to work on her listening skills. A girl of remarkable poten-tial, Stacy sometimes hands in her homework late and often talks in class. When she grows up, she would like to be a very famous comedian, but should that fail, she will be a plastic surgeon like her father, who has a practice in Purchase, New York, and a girlfriend who could be his business card. Her mother, Shelly, an obsessive knitter, has bad taste in dresses and inte-rior design and thinks that makeup is too "sophisti-cated" for a thirteen-year-old (might as well just round up) to wear. Shelly happens to be single and available for dates, in case any eligible men happen to be read-ing this wedding announcement. Stacy's ten-year-old brother, Arthur, is as tall as a nineteen-year-old and has an IQ of 160. Needless to say, having a taller and *smarter-than-you baby brother is mortifying in ways this wedding announcement can't adequately express.*

The bridegroom, thirteen, is also a member of the seventh grade at the Rye Country Day School in Rye, New York, where he is the captain of the junior varsity soccer team and the manager of the tennis team. Andrew is also a trendsetter in his grade, bringing to the classroom his flair for hip-hop through culture and language. Andrew plans on becoming either a music video director or a soccer coach when he grows up. In addition to the soccer team, he is on the baseball team, and when he gets to high school, he would like very much to be on the wrestling team, but soccer is his first love; after all, he has just gotten the same haircut as Lionel Messi, which happens to look incredibly sexy on him.

His mother teaches Hebrew at the congregation Emanu-El of Westchester. His father is the owner of Goldfarb Imports, a diamond concern. He has two older sisters, who pretend he doesn't exist, but they will feel sorry about that when he is on national TV playing for Real Madrid, with his wife, Stacy Adelaide Friedman, cheering for him in the stands.

The couple plans to honeymoon for four weeks in Hawaii, where Andy will finally tell Stacy the nature of the secret pact that he had with Lydia Katz. After that, the couple plans to live happily ever after and have three to eight children.

26.
The Taming of the Jew

I ran to the window when I heard my mother scream-ing. I looked out and saw Arthur splayed out on his back on the grass, arms to his sides and legs out like he was making a snow angel. Dante was standing over my mother, who was kneeling over Arthur.

"Arthur! Arthur!" Mom yelled, and slapped his cheeks as he slowly came to.

"What happened?" she turned around and asked Dante.

"He took too much air. Then went boom."

"Well, what were you doing with him?" she demanded.

"Making exercise."

"What?" she asked, then looked up as I came flying out the front door.

"He's helping Arthur to get coordinated," I called as I ran toward them.

My mother's face softened. Arthur sat up and looked around, confused. Then my mother looked up at Dante and smiled as if she were staring at a movie star.

"That is just about the loveliest thing I've ever heard. You are a dear, sweet boy," she said to Dante.

Hey, lady! This was all my idea.

"It is my pleasure for helping Arthur to become more in touch with his body rhythmics."

Dante extended his beautifully bronzed hand toward Arthur, who grabbed it. Dante pulled him up in one swift move. Wow. That was strength. Even Arthur looked astonished.

"Maybe that's enough for today," he said to Dante.

"Tomorrow, then?" Dante asked.

"That is accurate," Arthur answered. Dante patted Arthur on the shoulder like he was a friend, like he wasn't embarrassed to be seen with him. Then he leaned over and kissed my mother on each cheek, did the same to me, and then shook Arthur's hand goodbye. We stood there staring as he mounted his bike. Boy, was Andy lucky that Dante was so out of my league.

"What a lovely, lovely boy," my mother said about Dante as he left.

My mother and Arthur continued watching Dante as he disappeared down our driveway on his bike. Their eyes misted over as if they were gazing at one of the Seven Wonders of the World. I wanted to snap my fingers and jolt them out of it, but I had to admit, it was a pretty funny sight.

27.
Oh, What a Larder

Two days before MY BAT MITZVAH, I bought some tights to wear with my new dusty-pink tulle dress. As I walked home from the Duane Reade near my house, Alan Weiss pulled up with Dante in the car. Dante's host father was taking him over for a session with Arthur, so they gave me a lift. What a nice host father!

We pulled up to the driveway and my mother was outside. She was out of her knitting chair. I couldn't believe it. She must have decided the scarf was finally long enough.

She was pruning the hedges and had a touch of color on her sunken cheeks. She wore oversized sunglasses, and her hair was pulled back in a scarf. She looked accidentally very chic.

Please, God, let her have showered.

"My word. I can't believe it. That's the woman," Alan said.

"What woman?" I asked.

"The beautiful one from the mall," he said.

Beautiful?

"You mean my mother?" I asked, stunned.

"That's your mother? I thought she was the other girl's mother," he said, and dashed out of the car so quickly he didn't even shut the door behind him. He just walked straight over to my mother and introduced himself. Dante and I sat in the back seat, looking at each other.

"Dante?" I asked, realizing Dante may have some inside intel about Lydia and Andy.

"Yes, Stacy."

"Do you know anything about a pact?"

"A pack?"

"Yes."

"Like a pack-pack?"

"A pack-pack?"

"Yes, to carry books on your back."

"Oh. You mean a backpack. No, I'm talking about a pact, like the kind that two people have together. Like a secret agreement. Do you know of two people in our class who have a pact?"

"I don't think so. I don't believe in secrets. Sorry, Stacy, I know nothing of pacts."

I really wanted to know what the pact was before I saw Andy at my bat mitzvah on Saturday. Just in case it somehow affected my plan to make him my boyfriend.

We got out of the car, and my mom and Alan Weiss were still shaking hands.

"We're going to find Arthur," I called out to them.

But they didn't even turn around.

We followed the music and saw Arthur on the basketball court with a surprising amount of coordination for someone who basically tripped over air. He was dancing, not the way Dante had been teaching him, but like someone trying to walk through a Category 5 hurricane. We watched him for a minute without him seeing us and giggled behind a tree. And then he looked up and saw us.

"That's my warm-up," Arthur announced proudly.

"Your warm-up looks like you're battling a flesh-eating disease," I said.

"You mean necrotizing fasciitis?"

"Excuse me?" I asked.

"Flesh-eating disease is the common name for necrotizing fasciitis," Arthur said with a roll of the eyes.

"I will come find you when we finish our fun!" Dante called to me as I ran off to check on my mom.

My mother and Mr. Weiss weren't in the driveway anymore, but his car was still there. I heard laughter in the kitchen, and I stepped into the hallway to eavesdrop a bit.

"So then once you have the cucumbers washed, you'll want to cut them and place them in the vinegar to pickle," my mom said.

"And how long does that take?" Mr. Weiss asked.

"Well, depends how pickled you want your pickles."

Peals of laughter floated through the kitchen door.

"Really, it's a stunning larder," Alan said.

My poor mother. How was she ever going to land a man if her flirting technique involved showing them her larder? Poor Alan Weiss wasn't long for this world.

28.
Something Straight This Way Comes

Dear God, here is a list of all the good deeds I've done today:

1. *Put the shower faucet in the DOWN position like my mother likes it.*
2. *Put my clothes in the hamper.*
3. *Put the lids back on the ice-cream containers.*
4. *Put the ice-cream containers back into the freezer.*

5. *Folded my towels before hanging them back on the rack.*
6. *Said thank you when Arthur gave me the remote control.*
7. *Thought about trying one of my mother's cigarettes but did not try one of my mother's cigarettes.*
8. *And finally, I made my bed. FOR THE SECOND DAY IN A ROW!*

It was the day before my bat mitzvah. I was a wreck. I had failed miserably at completing my mitzvahs, and while I certainly wasn't expecting rewards anymore, I had to admit, deep inside I was still hoping to be gifted somehow for my efforts.

That evening the hair lady came over. She liked to work on hair the day before an event because as everyone knows, it always looks best the second day. Kelly came over to watch.

I'd never discussed my hair with the lady; I was planning on just leaving it in her hands. Which was a really good move because she did something no one has ever done to me in my entire life.

SHE.
STRAIGHTENED.
MY.
HAIR.

I have never felt more beautiful than I did that first moment that I got up from my desk chair, where the lady had been working on me, and looked at myself in my bathroom mirror. My hair was thick and shiny and looked darker somehow—almost black—and it fell down my back like it had a purpose. When I walked, it swung. When I put it behind my ears, it stayed there. It did exactly what I told it to do. I wanted to do cartwheels just to watch my *straight* hair sweep the grass. And flip over when I stood back up. There was no frizz, no cartoon-scribble drawing on top of my head. This was hair. By the power vested in me, you, lady of the ionic ceramic straightening iron, are my savior!

Just as I was imagining Andy's face lighting up when he saw me like this, I was seized by a very real terror that he wouldn't show. I mean, there was no guarantee that he'd remember or that he'd even want to go to a party where Lydia might be. For all he knew, I had re-invited her to my bat mitzvah. How could I make sure that Andy would come, see my gorgeousness, and fall in love with me?

I turned to Kelly.

"Do you think Andy is going to come tomorrow?" I asked.

"Of course. Unless you uninvited him also."

"No, he's still invited. But what if he thinks he's not?"

"He'll be there," Kelly said.

She seemed very certain of this fact. But I wasn't. So, when Kelly went to the kitchen for a snack, I called Andy to make sure he knew to come tomorrow. I used Kelly's cell phone and dialed, but when he picked up the phone and said, "Whaddup, sis?" I was so afraid, I hung up.

STACY FRIEDMAN'S RULES FOR PHONE ANXIETY: When calling someone who you really want to talk to, SAY SOMETHING WHEN THEY PICK UP!

Way to go, self.

29.
Oy Mitzvah!

*Okay, God, this is it. The big day. The
one I've been dreading and anticipating.
I can't ask you to do anything you
don't believe is in my best interest, and
I really don't know what to make of
your thoughts on this Andy situation,
but I'm asking you, (almost) adult
to adult, to allow me one moment,
just one second of happiness, in the
arms of the boy who is meant to be*

my first kiss. Please, send him to me.
And also, God, I understand that all
the little good deeds I've been doing
don't exactly add up to even one real
mitzvah, but if I keep at it, maybe the
final tally will add up. So maybe you'd
consider awarding me some credit?

The morning of my bat mitzvah did not start out well. I dreamed that I had agreed to four hundred mitzvahs and that I had forgotten about the agreement until ten minutes before I was to arrive at the bimah.

I was so flustered by my dream that I got out of bed immediately when I woke up, jumped over Kelly as she slept below in the trundle bed, ran downstairs, and started doing as many good deeds as possible.

I made Arthur a bowl of cereal, but then he didn't want it.

"I'm off carbs," he said as he cracked a raw egg into a glass and downed the whole thing in one gulp.

I made my mother more coffee (not that she needed it). Well, I tried. But the coffee looked like hot water with brown crayon mixed in and it overflowed the pot. She just said, "Thanks for trying," and shooed me upstairs to get ready as she cleaned up the mess I'd made.

Everything I tried to do backfired. I wondered if it was a sign.

Okay, I get it, God, but what are you trying to tell me?

STACY FRIEDMAN'S RULES FOR READING OMENS: When and if someone sends a sign (especially if this someone is God), the sign should be decipherable. If it is not decipherable, just pretend the omen is good. Even if it's not.

My stomach not only had butterflies as I got ready, it had fish and caterpillars and just about every crawly thing imaginable. I recited my Torah portion in my head at least forty-seven times. I practiced singing quietly, but all I could hear were the cracks in my voice and my congenital amusia. I was mortified in front of myself. My palms were sweaty and I wasn't sure if I was more nervous about Andy watching me all dressed up and singing and being the center of attention, or for the actual bat mitzvah.

And then an even worse thought occurred to me.

I turned to Kelly, who still hadn't gotten out of bed, and said, "He's not going to come."

Without even opening her eyes she said, "Yes, he is."

Then I put on a shower cap (couldn't risk curling up my newly straightened hair) and jumped in the shower, and when I got out, I could hear Kelly talking to someone in my room.

"Who was that?" I asked as I entered my room.

"Who was who?" she asked.

"On the phone?"

"I wasn't on the phone," she said.

"Kelly, I just heard you talking."

"You're losing it, sister," she said.

She was right about that.

I zipped up my dress and Kelly played some music to calm me down, and then raced to feed herself. I was rifling through Kelly's makeup bag when my mom came in.

"Someone called for a final touch-up?" she said, holding a tube of a lipstick so pale, it might as well have been ChapStick. I smiled, and she gently held my chin as she applied the lipstick.

She looked so pretty. Was she—gasp—actually wearing makeup? By Shelly, I think she was!

"I can't believe your big day is finally here," she said.

"I know, right?"

"And look how grown-up you are! You're not a little girl anymore."

She turned me around and we both looked at each other in the full-length mirror. I looked zero different than before she applied the lipstick.

"No matter how old you are, to me, you'll always be every age you've ever been."

I smiled, imagining a fast montage of myself from swaddled infant to now, as Kelly raced back in.

"What did I miss?" she asked.

"Not a thing," my mom said. "Downstairs in ten, okay?" she asked as she headed out of my room.

Kelly waited until my mom was completely out of sight before grabbing her makeup bag to go over my face with a somewhat heavier hand, including black mascara (which would hopefully go undetected by my mother), and when I turned back to the mirror, I barely recognized myself. I actually looked pretty. No, scratch that. I looked, well, kind of beautiful. Not 40 percent or even 50 percent more beautiful, but 100 percent more beautiful.

Kelly said, "Wow. Andy Goldfarb is going to have to remind himself to keep blinking. You are that gorgeous."

I almost cried from this compliment, but I didn't. Mascara.

"It doesn't matter. I'm telling you. He's not coming," I told her.

"Hey, Stace. Remember before when I wasn't on the phone?"

"Yeah," I said.

"Well, the person I wasn't on the phone with was Andy," she said, and smiled.

"What did you say to him?" I asked, panicking.

"Don't worry. I just called to say I was taking requests for the DJ," she said proudly.

"Very smart, sister," I said. "He didn't mention anything about a pact, did he?"

"Nada," she said.

I jumped up and down for joy. I was so happy, I couldn't believe it! He really was coming!

I heard a car pull up on the gravel of our driveway.

When I ran to the window, I saw that it was Alan Weiss's car. That was strange, I thought. Maybe Dante forgot that today was my bat mitzvah, which meant no lessons for Arthur. I ran downstairs to tell him. Both my mom and Arthur were at the bottom of the stairs, and as I walked down, they both looked up. My mother gasped. Arthur smiled.

"Wow. Look at you, Stacy Friedman. You are magnificent," my mother said.

"That is accurate," Arthur agreed. "You clean up nice."

I think I must have been blushing. For the first time in my life, I felt beautiful. I have to say, my mom looked pretty great herself. And as for Arthur, I almost cried when I saw him. He was an absolute vision in his tuxedo. In fact, he hadn't asked anyone to help him get into it, so he was incrementally more coordinated! Mitzvah number one was officially complete. And that felt so much better than I had ever imagined it would.

"You guys aren't too shabby yourselves," I said, giving them each a friendly little pat on the shoulders. "I'll be right back. I have to tell Dante that Arthur's lessons are finished," I called as I reached the bottom of the stairs.

"Oh, honey, he's not here for a lesson. They're driving us. He's going as my date," my mother said.

"Dante?" I asked, incredulous.

"No, sweetheart." My mom laughed. "Alan. We're going to your bat mitzvah together."

I couldn't believe my earholes. My mother was going on a date. She wouldn't be alone at my bat mitzvah! She wouldn't have to deal with my father and Delilah all by herself. I was amazed. Not only at my mother's stunning turnaround, but also at the fact that two of my mitzvahs were now suddenly and unexpectedly complete.

I mean, sure, my mom and Alan found each other on their own. But I was the one who invited Dante over (as an act of loving kindness, no less) and I was the one who put the idea of dating in my mother's head. So I felt it counted as my mitzvah fair and square. I was on a roll now. Who knew? Maybe by the time I got to the synagogue, the third one would magically be completed too.

Kelly came careening down the stairs and we all

went outside, where Dante and Alan were waiting. Dante's eyebrows shot up when he saw me.

"Your hair—it changed," he said, sounding surprised.

"It's so much better, right?" I asked.

"Not better. Different. I like your hair before with all the curls."

He did?

"But I like you with flat hair too."

I smiled at him, pleased.

My mother took pictures of us kids, and when she finished, Dante bowed, which I thought was both funny and cute. Then he stood next to me and put his hand on his waist so I could put my arm through his. I did and he led me to the car. I looked up at him and for a moment I let myself wonder what it would be like to be his girlfriend. But that was ridiculous. Dante was out of my league. Plus, he already had a girlfriend at home *and* a bikini model here. Maybe even others.

He sure was attentive, though.

But, God, he's well out of my league—right?

Perhaps it was just reflex, but I swear I heard a God-voice inside my head: *"Inaccurate."*

30.
A Torah & a Haftarah
Walk into a Bar...

I waited inside Rabbi Sherwin's office until it was time to read from the Torah. The third mitzvah had not been completed, magically or otherwise. I was a nervous wreck. I bit my fingernails; I twirled my hair (but then I realized that would just make it curly again, so I stopped). I looked for some more good deeds to do. I cleaned the dirt from between Rabbi's laptop keys; I pulled the next Kleenex slightly out of its box so he wouldn't have to dig in for it; I located four stray Hershey's Kiss wrappers underneath the chair and I put them all in the trash, and six unopened ones scattered on his desk, which I collected into one pile. If Lydia had been there, we'd have eaten at least two of the chocolates, if not all; but without her, I just wasn't tempted.

Then I heard the rustling and murmurs of guests piling into the synagogue, so I dropped the good deeds to wedge my face through the crack in the door to watch. I saw Megan and Sara looking for their seats. Kelly was sitting with her parents behind my mother and Arthur. My dad was there with his statue. Dante and his father were next to my mother and Arthur. I craned my neck farther to find Andy, but I didn't see him anywhere.

Soon Rabbi Sherwin entered the room.

"Seema? Are you ready?"

"I think so," I said. I was so not ready.

"Then let's go show these people what you've got."

I was halfway through the first line of the Torah portion (doing a fine job, I think, for someone with congenital amusia) when I spotted Kym.

Kym!

Who did she think she was, showing up when I had

uninvited her? You can't just go around ignoring uninvitations. Can you?

That made my blood boil, but then I wondered if maybe Lydia also ignored my uninvitation. Actually, I couldn't tell if I was wondering about Lydia or hoping. Not that it mattered; she definitely wasn't there.

I got through the portion without puncturing anyone's eardrums, and it was time for my speech. I was shaking a little bit, but right as I was about to begin, I saw some odd movement off to the side. At first I wouldn't allow myself to believe what my eyes were telling me, but it was undeniable. Kym was sticking a tissue up her nose. Not just in it, but up it. Just digging away with it as if it mattered that there was a tissue in between her fingers and her nostril. Like she was in the privacy of her own bathroom rather than a very public and, might I add, holy place. I almost laughed out loud, but I swallowed it. Too bad Lydia wasn't there; she would have thought it was the funniest.

Ugh, why did I keep thinking about Lydia?

"Today is a very important day in my life. It's the day I become an adult and take on adult responsibilities," I said, and then paused for a minute.

My mother was beaming. Kelly was smiling. Arthur was studying Dante. My dad winked proudly at me and clutched Delilah's hand. And then I finally spotted Andy. No wonder he was so hard to find—he was seated in the absolute back row, with his head down. His shoulders were wiggling oddly. He was texting! Why wasn't he focused on me?

"As an adult, I have adult responsibilities, and with these adult responsibilities comes...comes..." I was stumped. I looked down at my speech and realized what a hypocrite I was. Here I was proclaiming that I was an adult with the ability to make right and holy choices and I had chosen a boy over my best friend. And he wasn't even really that nice to me or attentive. I mean, I was standing right in front of him, all made up, with my hair all glossy straight, with my new dress on, and what was he doing? Texting! Dante barely spoke English, and when I looked over at him, he was paying more attention to my speech than Andy Goldfarb was. I had given Lydia up for *that*?

I looked again at the crowd. Everyone was waiting for me to finish my speech. So I went with what I had. "And with these responsibilities comes the privilege of calling oneself a full-fledged member of the Jewish community. Sometimes there are sacrifices that need to be made..." I continued, noticing maybe for the first time how beautiful the temple was. The way the stained glass reflected the sun rays, dividing them into beautiful colors and warming the room. The outside smell of cut grass and morning dew seeped in. This was a precious moment in my life, and the person who mattered most (well, except maybe my family) wasn't there to share it with me. Something had to be done.

"I'm sorry. I am standing here telling you about adult responsibility when in reality I don't know anything about being an adult. If I knew about being grown-up, I would have done what I'm about to do a long time ago," I said. The audience shifted in confusion as I grabbed my cell phone out of my purse.

"So if you'll excuse me, I really have to make a phone call." Just as my scrolling finger landed on Lydia's name, my mother called out from her seat, "Stacy! Put down that phone."

"No, Mom," I said. "I have to do this."

She got up out of her seat and headed up the stage steps toward me.

"This is not the time to make phone calls, young lady," she hissed.

"Actually, it is the perfect time," I responded.

My mother looked at Rabbi Sherwin, who looked at me.

"Rabbi Sherwin, please. It's important," I pleaded.

Rabbi Sherwin looked up and studied the stained-glass windows. There was absolute silence in the synagogue as we awaited the verdict. With his eyes closed and his face pointed toward the windows, he pursed his lips and arrived at a decision.

"Let Stacy make her own choices today," he said.

I smiled broadly at him and pressed call.

Lydia picked up on the first ring.

"Hello?" she said.

"Lydia?" I spoke into the phone and heard her name echo in the synagogue while all eyes were on me.

"Stacy?" she asked.

Even though I was standing on a stage, I needed a little privacy. So I walked to the edge of the stage and covered my mouth with my hand. I loud-whispered into the phone.

"I've made a terrible mistake. I am standing at the bimah, looking into the audience trying to find you and you're not here. I mean, of course you're not here; I told you not to come. The point is that I've imagined this day for a long time, but in my imagination you were always here." At this next part, I whispered even softer. "Even Kym is here and she was uninvited also!" Then in a normal voice I said, "I can't finish this day without you. I take back what I said. Even though you *have* been behaving in a totally gruesome manner, I know you are going to explain everything to me and it will somehow make sense. You are SO invited to my bat mitzvah."

"Really?" she said, excited.

"Yeah. Do you still have that Stella McCartney dress? Even though we haven't been speaking, it occurred to me the other day that it would look really good with your London Sole shoes."

"Yeah, it would. But actually, I just bought a new pair that would go even better!" Lydia said.

"You did?" I asked, momentarily upset that she had new fashion purchases I didn't know about. "What color are they?"

My mother made a throat-clearing noise, and I looked up and realized this was not the sort of conversation I was supposed to be having during my bat mitzvah speech.

"I have to go now," I said without even giving her the chance to answer my question. "But you'll come, right?"

"I wouldn't miss it for the world."

I hung up, looked at the audience, and felt more like an adult than I ever had. And then it dawned on me. Re-inviting Lydia to my bat mitzvah was my third mitzvah. I actually had done something worthwhile and I wasn't even thinking about the rewards! I wanted her there because I loved her, and I forgave her because friendship was worth more than Andy Goldfarb.

"I guess I should explain," I said to the audience.

How exactly was I going to explain this? I tried to sort out the important details and just deliver the facts, but then I thought, no—I am an adult; I should just be honest and give it to them straight.

"Since the theme of my Torah portion is sacrifice, I was going to make this really boring speech about what people should give up and what people should hold on to. But who am I really to talk about sacrifice when I have only been thinking of myself?"

This was becoming too lecturey. I took a deep breath and started over. Dante was smiling brightly at me, and it weirdly calmed me down.

"Okay, I'm going to level with you. There was this boy, right? And I really truly liked him, even though I could barely understand a word he said, not because he was from another country or anything, but because he was from another planet. No, that's not right either. There's a boy who I thought was cool based on superficial reasons alone. I thought he was really cute, but I've learned that it's what people do that matters most. Actions are a language that communicates feelings, and when you show up for someone but then don't pay attention"—I looked right at Andy to see if any of this was sinking in, but of course it wasn't because he was looking at his phone—"or you lead people to believe you like them only to push them away in public, then you are communicating who you are as a person.

"I overlooked the signals because he was so cute. But he plays games and isn't very honest or considerate, unlike other boys, who I am discovering can actually be very attentive and thoughtful. Anyway, the long and short of it is that I caught my best friend kissing the boy I liked and felt betrayed even though he wasn't my boyfriend to begin with. Are you guys following this?"

Andy wasn't looking at his phone anymore. But I

was no longer interested in looking at him. Instead, I took in the front row. Some people nodded, even Delilah. Kelly gave me a thumbs-up. Dante had a confused smile on his face. Arthur leaned forward, reached into his pocket, and pulled out a carrot stick. Then he bit into it and listened carefully.

"So I uninvited my best friend from the most important day of my life and decided to exact revenge on her, making her life as miserable as she made mine.

"Then Rabbi Sherwin suggested that maybe revenge wasn't really the best way to go about things. He advised me to perform three mitzvahs before my bat mitzvah in order to learn sacrifice and selflessness, you know, all the things my Torah portion was about. But I didn't really get it. The selfish part of me thought that if I just performed these three mitzvahs, then the boy I liked would like me back.

"Not that it mattered. I didn't really succeed in the whole mitzvah business anyway. I could only think of two people to perform mitzvahs for, but it wasn't them I was concerned about. It was me. When I left my house this morning, I still had one whole mitzvah that I hadn't even started. It was only when I got to the bimah and called my best friend that I ended up performing the last mitzvah, which ironically also turned out to be my first.

"I guess sacrifice isn't about getting rewarded. The reward is the feeling you get by giving of yourself. Being able to help someone else *is* the gift. That's what being Jewish means."

The audience was silent. I just stood there with my straightened hair and in my okay but not great bat mitzvah outfit. And then finally, I said, "Well, that's pretty much all I have to say. I guess—well—I guess since we're all here anyway, and I'm on a stage, I'll end this on a joke." I paused and looked at my mom, who did not look happy about this last addition, and then at Rabbi Sherwin, who shrugged and smirked. But you know what? It was my day. I had sung my Torah portion without laughing; I tried to repair the world. It was time for a little comic relief, people. And so, I began.

"So this guy is relaxing, watching TV one night, and he hears a banging on the door. He gets up, goes to the door, opens it, looks out, doesn't see anyone, shrugs, closes the door, and goes back to his show. A few minutes later, he hears the knock again. Same thing: nobody there. By the fourth time of getting up, he's pretty annoyed, but when he opens the door, he glances down and happens to see a snail in front of the door on the welcome mat. Angry at being disturbed, he picks up the snail and flings it across the street into an open field. Three years later, there's a loud banging on the door and he opens it again to find the snail there. The snail says, 'So what the heck was that all about?'"

The audience let out a big laugh and then they erupted like it was a sporting event. They cheered and clapped and Rabbi Sherwin mouthed something to me that I couldn't decipher, but I'm pretty sure it had the word *grown-up* in it. Then the entire congregation got to their feet and gave me a standing ovation. My first ever. But hopefully not my last.

I looked over at my mother and she was beaming at me. Then I crumpled up my speech and looked out at the audience. I felt confident, I felt mature, and I felt adult. I had delivered a speech I hadn't even written and I meant every last word of it. And I did stand-up, live, from a real stage—and you know what, folks? I killed!

31.
Work It

Kids were jumping on trampolines, eating candy apples and cotton candy spun on the premises. Stilt walkers, jugglers, and contortionists roamed about and a DJ played great music and took requests. My dad was being sunk over and over again in the ball toss, and there was already a line for the miniature moonwalk. Everyone seemed to be having an amazing time. I couldn't believe we had actually pulled it off.

Some boys were on one side of the dance floor and

some girls were on the other and all parents were in an adjoining room, drinking coffee (*thank you, God!*).

The only downside was that no one was dancing. Arthur looked miserable by himself in the corner. His eyes were glued to Sara Langley, but she wouldn't even look at him. Finally, Dante got up on the dance floor. Everyone circled him as he did his usual explosive moves. People were clapping and screaming and finally Dante called for Arthur. Looking panicked, Arthur shook his head. But Dante didn't give up so easily and soon Arthur gave in. The crowd parted to let him through, and then created a circle around my little tall brother. Arthur stood there kind of dumbstruck for a minute.

The music changed, and when Missy Elliott's "Work It" came out of the speakers, Arthur's face suddenly changed from terrified to ecstatic. He lit up and slowly let the music take him over. A calmness came over his face and he began to move. And boy, could the formerly gangly, uncoordinated kid move. Halfway through the song, he was moving like a professional backup dancer. Hallelujah, the boy was good! We all started clapping for him and cheering him on. Pretty soon, we were all dancing too.

Who'd have ever thought that Arthur Saul Friedman of all people could get a dance party started?

Dante started dancing with Arthur. Dante would do a move, then Arthur would mirror it back. Then Arthur would do a move and Dante would mirror it back. It was really touching to watch. Arthur idolized him.

Andy came out on the dance floor too. But to call what he was doing dancing would be a huge stretch. He didn't even move his legs. He just kept crossing and uncrossing his arms and bending the top part of his body over like an old man trying to hug a child who wasn't there. It was painful. Especially when I looked over at Dante to compare the two. Watching him as he danced made my heart skip a beat. When I realized that he was looking back at me, I think it actually stopped.

And then I realized that Dante was making his way over to me.

Dante stood next to me without saying anything. When the next song started, he leaned over.

"You like this song?" Dante asked.

"Yeah, it's great," I said.

"Do you like to dance?" he asked.

"Oh, I love to dance," I answered.

"I didn't know. Perhaps you would like—"

"Stacy!" I heard a girl's voice calling to me.

There, in her Stella McCartney dress, was Lydia. I ran toward her. Once I got there, I didn't know what to say to her. She didn't seem to know what to say to me either, so we both just stared at each other in silence. Finally, I said, "I just need to know one thing. I need to know why you kissed Andy when you knew I liked him."

"You said you were over him," she said, her face completely innocent.

"But I wasn't," I contended. "I mean, it's not like crushes go away overnight, and at least you could have checked with me or something."

"I guess when you renounced him, I just took you at your word," she said.

"But you didn't even have a crush on him."

"Well, I didn't—at first. But then at the quarry, Kym kept on making fun of me for not liking boys, so when I went swimming, Andy and I got left alone for a minute and I asked him if maybe one day we could try kissing so I would know what it was like and could say that I *had* kissed a boy. He agreed and invited me over to his house so we could try it, and when we tried it, I don't know what happened. I think I just, like, fell in love with him or something."

"What was the pact?"

"How'd you know about that?" she asked.

"I overheard you two in the library."

"Oh," she said, saddened. "Yeah. We had a pact that we would practice kissing in private. Never, ever in public. Anyway, it just so happened that the first time I went over to practice was also the day you saw us."

"That was the worst day of my life," I said.

"Mine too," she replied, and my heart actually went out to her. Of course she'd fallen in love with Andy Goldfarb through some kind of magic kissing spell. I hadn't even kissed him, and I had fallen for it. But then I thought about how rude it was to only kiss someone in private. Lydia deserved to be kissed in public at the mall if she wanted to be! Even though that is something I would never advise.

"I'm still really upset that you did that to me," I said. But there was something even more important we had to talk about now: "So, did you like it?"

"Kissing?" she asked.

"Yeah."

"It was kind of weird. Like if you run your tongue over your teeth. It felt kind of like that. But he smelled like pizza!"

"Ewwwwww!" I said. "Are you still in love with him?" I asked.

"No way!" she said. "He's a total jerk."

"I wish you had told me all this earlier," I said.

"Well, I tried to talk to you at school, but you wouldn't let me."

"I know. I'm sorry about that," I said.

"I'm sorry too," she said.

"Do you promise never, ever to let a boy come between our friendship ever again?" I asked her.

"I do," she said. "Do you promise?"

"Of course I do!" I said.

And then she handed me a present. "Congratulations on your bat mitzvah."

I opened it up. It was the perfect gold pleated dress I had gotten stuck in that day at the Galleria. But in the right size!

"I know it's too late to wear it for your bat mitzvah, but maybe you can wear it to mine."

"How did you know about this?"

"Kelly told me what happened in the store that day."

"I can't wait to try it on when I get home," I said, hugging her. When I let go, she said, "One more thing." She handed me a small bubble-wrapped envelope that I opened, and inside was my half of our friendship necklace. I put the necklace over my head and then I burst into tears. It just crept up on me without any of the usual warning signals. When Lydia saw me crying, she started crying too. Then we hugged.

"You better stop crying before the dampness from your tears makes your hair frizz up," she said. Which made me laugh really hard. Which made her laugh really hard. We were laughing and crying at the same time, which was so funny that the laughing eventually overtook the crying.

"Come on, you, you won't believe how good Arthur is at dancing!" I said, grabbing Lydia's hand and running to the dance floor.

Dante walked back over to us.

"You are friends again?" he asked.

We both nodded, beaming ear to ear. I think we were so happy, we could barely speak. Just then Kelly ran over to us.

"Check out how bad a dancer Andy is," she said.

"The worst," Lydia agreed.

"Boom Clap" by Charli XCX came on and I noticed how antsy Dante was being next to me. He kept on jiggling his leg like he had to go to the bathroom. I was looking up at him, about to ask if he was okay, when he said, "This is a good song, yes?"

"Yeah. I love this song," I said.

"It is fun dancing to also," he said to me.

"Probably," I said.

"You have never danced to this song before?" he asked.

"Not in public."

He was about to say something else when we heard the clinking of glass. It was my mother. The music stopped and everyone went silent and turned in her direction. I held on to Lydia's and Kelly's hands for this cringeworthy moment.

STACY FRIEDMAN'S RULE FOR TOASTING: When toasting your daughter at her bat mitzvah, make it snappy.

"This is not going to be a long toast," my mother said. Finally! She had learned a rule.

"Stacy Adelaide Friedman is no ordinary girl. Today we have collectively witnessed what a profoundly good friend Stacy is. She is also a wonderful sister and daughter. I am proud to have her in my corner. Mazel tov to you, Stacy, on your special day!"

Okay, I admit it. I got a little weepy on that one. My mother called me profound. Raising me has been rewarding for her. Who knew?

I gave my mother a hug and a big kiss and told her I loved her. And right after I kissed her, Alan, Dante's father host, leaned over and kissed her also. On the cheek. Not on the mouth. *Thank you, God.*

The music started again. This time it was a slower song—Paris Paloma's "It's Called: Freefall." Alan took my mother's hand and led her out onto the dance floor. Delilah and my father followed. Then Rabbi Sherwin and his wife, Annie, walked out onto the dance floor. All the old people were slow dancing. It was kind of embarrassing and sweet at the same time.

Then Kelly pinched the back of my arm. "You will NOT believe what is happening right now." She turned us toward the dance floor, where Arthur was speaking to Sara Langley.

"My hand-eye coordination has been achieved and perfected!" I overheard him saying.

Uh-oh. I had forgotten about that lie I had told him.

"Cool," Sara Langley said.

"That's what you said you wanted," he told her.

She looked confused and at a loss for words, but when he extended his hand to her, she actually took it, and together they went to the dance floor. Which was a really sweet thing for her to do. And really lucky for me because I was one minute away from being caught in a lie.

Just then Kelly turned and put her arm around both Lydia and me.

"Oh my God! I just realized! You guys are finally speaking. Are we all friends again?" she asked.

"Always," Lydia and I said together. Then we walked over to the cotton candy machine and waited for the lady to make us three cones. Dante came over and stood with us. "This is like sugarcane?" he asked.

"No, more like just sugar," I said.

The woman handed me a paper cone and I offered Dante a batch. He took it, and when he put it in his mouth, his eyes lit up.

"Delicious," he said. And then, "Stacy?"

"Yeah?"

"I been wanting to know something now for a few whiles."

"What?"

He looked around, pumped his leg up and down nervously, looked at the floor, and finally asked, "Will you dance with me?"

"Me?" I asked.

"Yes. You."

"Yeah. Okay. Sure," I said as I handed my cotton candy to Lydia. Then, with just our eyes, she said, "Omg!" and I responded, "Right?! What is happening?" before I turned back to Dante.

"You've been wanting to dance with me this whole time?" I asked as I walked him to the dance floor.

"Yes."

"But why didn't you ask me?" I said, mostly to make sure he was in fact saying what I thought he was saying.

"I tried. But you didn't hear me," he said, laughing nervously.

I was very confused by his behavior. Why on earth would Dante Decosimo want to dance with me?

I had never danced to a slow song before, but I guess he had, because he put his arm around my back. Then I put my head on his chest like all the girls in movies do. I was sweating and nervous. What did this mean? I had never been this close to a boy before in my entire life. I could actually smell him. I had goose bumps. And *they* had goose bumps.

Dante pulled away for a minute and looked at me. I tried my hardest not to get my hopes up. I told myself he was just going to ask me if having a bat mitzvah was fun or if we could get more cotton candy when we finished dancing. And I forced myself to believe it.

"Stacy?" he asked me.

"Yes, Dante?"

"A kiss would be for me a lovely pleasure."

Did he mean on the cheek or a for-real kiss?

"You want to kiss me?" I asked.

"Since for a long time now," he said.

"Really?" I asked.

"Really, but you were loving Andy."

He leaned in and I closed my eyes because that's also what all the girls do in movies. Then I felt his lips on my lips. I was kissing a boy, right there in front of everyone on the dance floor at my bat mitzvah! And not only that, I was kissing Dante Decosimo! The most beautiful boy in the entire school. I, Stacy Adelaide Friedman, managed, after all, to have my first real kiss at my bat mitzvah. And it was good.

When the song ended, I ran over to Lydia and Kelly, who were standing on the edge of the dance floor.

"Oh my God!" Lydia said.

"That kiss was movie worthy!" Kelly said.

"You guys saw it?!" I asked.

"Yes!" they both said.

"It was amazing," I told them.

Dante Decosimo. Dante Decosimo. Dante Decosimo. I couldn't believe it! A boy who could dance! A boy who wasn't obsessed with soccer! A boy who was interesting! A boy who put a fancy handkerchief on my scraped knee! A boy who I always understood perfectly even though English wasn't his first language. A boy who didn't steal from other cultures to mask that he had no personality of his own! I could hardly believe it. It was entirely possible that I had myself an honest-to-goodness boyfriend.

32.
Never Tear Us Apart

Kelly, Lydia, and I stood in a corner of the party hall so that I could give them all the details of the Dante story. They let me tell it to them at least ten times.

Finally, Kelly said, "Can we change the subject for just a second to discuss Andy Goldfarb? Is it safe to say that as far as he is concerned, all signs point to..."

And at the same time the three of us stuck our heads together and yelled "NO!"

"Good riddance," Lydia said. "He did nothing but tear us apart."

A little while later, as I was going to cut the cake, Andy came up to me.

"Um...listen, nephew had no clue you were crushin' on him, but now I do because you know, that mad crazy speech. So if you wanted, we could, like, try kissing, just to see if we like it. You know, like me and Lydia did. I mean, I'm not really even s'posed to go out with girls and my dad wants me to focus on soccer, but, like, I didn't know that the betties were even digging on me—"

I had to interrupt the boy.

"Andy. I don't mean to be rude. But someone needs to call you out for the way you talk—"

"Yo whatsup?"

"You're a white Jewish boy who goes to a private school in a wealthy suburb of NYC," I reminded him.

"Yeah, fam, I know."

Wow, he was not getting it. "It's called cultural appropriation. Google it."

Andy stood there, red-faced and stunned, as I walked away toward my cake. Not five minutes later I overheard Andy talking to Lydia. I admit I eavesdropped to make sure Lydia was being straight with me.

"Um…listen, nephew thought you understood about the pact and everything, but, like, maybe you didn't, and, like, that's cool. So, if you wanted to, like, have another pact with more kissing, we could do that, but I do need, like, time with soccer and stuff."

It was almost the same speech. And you know what my best friend, Lydia Katz, said to him? Nothing. That girl just walked away, toward me. Her best friend. She forever took her seat.

I looked around and saw Arthur teaching Sara some of his moves in the corner and soon Kym and Megan joined them. My little brother was actually, gasp, kind of, actually, maybe even cool.

Thank you, God!

Andy, hands in his oversized pants pockets, made his way over to Kelly.

"Wanna dance?" he asked.

"Um…no. Thank you," she said as she walked away. Lydia and I turned our backs on him. But we did watch him walk over to Megan, who shook her head, and then to Sara, who also seemed to be saying no. Finally, he headed over to Kym and we were all about to ignore this latest effort when, what do you know—he put his arm around her, and they walked away together. Lydia and I looked at each other, mouths dropped, and then started laughing. It was perfect. No two seventh graders deserved each other more.

Kelly came running back over, giggling.

"Look what I got," she said, and pulled a bottle of champagne from her bag.

"Where did you get that?" Lydia asked.

"The adults have a whole bar in the other room!" Kelly shrieked as she pulled out three champagne glasses as well.

"A toast!" Kelly said as she poured the champagne into the glasses and raised hers up in the air. "Today is Stacy Adelaide Friedman's bat mitzvah. And I think she is the funniest person alive." But just as she was about to take a sip, an adult hand swooped down and grabbed the bottle and all three glasses. That hand, of course, belonged to my mother.

"Not on my watch, young lady," she said. Unbelievable, that woman's radar.

I went to the kids' bar and brought back three Shirley Temples. Then it was Lydia's turn to make a toast.

"You and I have come a long way: from best friends

to best enemies to best friends again. I hope we are friends forever!" she said as she took a big gulp.

"Forever and ever," I answered. And then I raised my glass and said, "To friendship!"

"TO FRIENDSHIP!" Lydia and Kelly repeated. And with that, I knocked back my Shirley Temple. Even though it wasn't alcoholic, it was the first time I ever had one, so that was somewhat exciting. Okay, not really. But that was okay. The day had already been exciting enough.

33.
Thank You & Mazel Tov!

Dear God,

   *I didn't think you heard me. Can you
believe that? I thought that all my prayers
were being sent to your spam filter, but it
seems you were just accumulating them
in order to see me through. I feel like the
happiest grown-up-about-to-turn-thirteen-
year-old in the world. And I LOVE my
hair. The outfit is good too. I'm glad that
you decided Andy wasn't for me. Because*

honestly, I just couldn't get on board with his ignorance. I couldn't speak his language. Now, Italian? That I can speak.

Anyway, God, this is going to be short because I have a dance floor to get back to, a boy I need to start dating, and a best friend to catch up with, but I just wanted to thank you, you know, for... well... everything, really. My mom and Alan, my brother, my father, and all my amazing friends. And especially for Lydia and Kelly, my absolute first- and second-best friends.

Okay, fine, thanks for Delilah too. She makes my dad happy, so that's enough for me.

Okay, God, I'll talk to you later. I just wanted to thank you for doing all this for me. I really appreciate it. My bat mitzvah turned out to be amazing. Now, if only you could work on my ears. They're a little too big. And my nose. Maybe by my sweet sixteen? Well, we'll talk.

Okay?

Great.

Thank you. From one adult to another.

> *Love,*
>
> *Stacy Adelaide Friedman*

Acknowledgments
& Thanks

Thank you to the team at Alloy, especially Sara Shandler, Romy Golan, Josh Bank, Leslie Morgenstein, and Elysa Dutton. Farrin Jacobs and the team at Little, Brown Books for Young Readers, including Jen Graham, Martina Rethman, Gabrielle Chang, and Crystal Castro. Cody Brown, Jeni and Sorelle Indresano, Piper Weiss for letting me use her name, the Sterns, Stuarts, Rudikoffs, and Rubels, and my favorite Baronian. And yes, of course you, Busy Stern.

Thank you to Adam, Jackie, Sadie, and Sunny Sandler for choosing this book to make into a movie, and for making my time on set so unimaginably fun.

Thank you also to Sammi Cohen, Alison Peck, and all the good folks at Netflix and Happy Madison.

Lastly, I want to thank all the young actors who brought these characters (and new ones!) to life, especially: Dylan, Judd, Dean, Samantha, Zaara, Miya, and all the players.

About the Author

Fiona Rosenbloom was born and raised in New York. When she is not writing, she's either at home in the farmhouse she shares with a group of dear friends, their kids, and sixteen rescue animals, or playing shows throughout Europe with her band, Stars Without Makeup. If you fact-check this, you'll discover it's all made up, just like the name Fiona Rosenbloom, a pseudonym for a writer named Amanda, who lives in Brooklyn with her dog, Busy Stern (@busyinbk).